Praise for **A Small**

'Perhaps not since John Marsden.
such a powerful novel set against the backdrop of a sudden and
vivid Australian war . . . if you loved Meg Rosoff's *How I Live Now*
and Mark Haddon's *The Curious Incident of the Dog in the Night-
time*, you will be left breathless by this stunning novel.'
Canberra Times

' . . . a story of hope and a celebration of the worth of the individual'
Suite 101.com

' . . . a heartstring tugger full of wayward wisdom and
gentle sentiment'
Adelaide Advertiser

'Millard may well have carved a place for herself as one of
Australia's preeminent contemporary children's authors.'
Bookseller & Publisher

' . . . a beautiful story . . . this book is delightful and stands as a
testimony to the power of family, friendship and love'
Viewpoint

'Don't expect this book to be similar to Millard's tales of the Silk
Kingdom. This is very different, extraordinarily so, yet equally
beautiful. It is a stark, poignant and gripping story . . . And,
as always, Millard's text simply sings.'
Good Reading

'This is more than a story of a journey of survival for it is also a
story of despair and hope, love and sorrow, courage and frailty.
Millard . . . has created something exceptional.'
Reading Time

'This philosophical, appealing survival tale is simultaneously

A Small
Free Kiss
in the
Dark

A *Small Free Kiss in the Dark* was first published in the UK in 2011. It is being republished in 2017 by Old Barn Books Ltd as a celebration of Glenda Millard's shortlisting for the CILIP Carnegie Medal (for *The Stars at Oktober Bend*) and because we believe this well-loved Australian writer deserves to be much better known in the UK.

On its first publication, the Library Mice blog (www.librarymice. com) said of A *Small Free Kiss in the Dark*:

'Be prepared to be moved, enchanted, heartbroken and uplifted all at the same time by this wonderfully poignant novel.'

We hope that you will be swept away, as we were, by the beauty and the power of Glenda's writing. We have made no attempt to 'anglicise' the Australian idiom and hope that you will enjoy the discovery of a new Antipodean vocabulary.

Other titles by Glenda Millard available in the UK from Old Barn Books:
The Stars at Oktober Bend (long listed for the UKLA Award and shortlisted for the Carnegie Medal)

Pea Pod Lullaby (a picture book) with illustrator Stephen Michael King, available from September 2017.

Also available in the UK:
The Kingdom of Silk series
The Duck and the Darklings – a picture book, with illustrator Stephen Michael King

A Small Free Kiss in the Dark

GLENDA MILLARD

Old Barn
Books

AN OLD BARN BOOK

Copyright © Glenda Millard, 2009

First published by Allen & Unwin Australia in 2009
First published in the UK in 2011

This 2017 edition published by Old Barn Books Ltd
Warren Barn, West Sussex, RH20 1JW
www.oldbarnbooks.com
email: info@oldbarnbooks.com
Distributed by Bounce Sales & Marketing Ltd,
email: sales@bouncemarketing.co.uk

ISBN 9781910646076

Cover and text design by Lisa White
Typesetting for the UK edition by Eyelevel Design
Printed in the UK

10 9 8 7 6 5 4 3 2 1

For Douglas
G.M.

Contents

A fun park isn't the kind of place you'd expect to find a ballerina on a rainy afternoon. But that's where we found Tia. In the beginning I wished we never found her. Three was perfect: Billy and Max and me. We didn't need anyone else to look after, especially not a ballerina. Worse still, she had a baby. You couldn't choose just one; they came together, like a free sample of mayonnaise sticky-taped to a bag of salad leaves.

The girl didn't look like a ballerina when we found her. She just looked like a girl wearing a long red coat and black motorbike boots that were way too big for her skinny legs. Her skin was the colour of the moon and her long hair blew around her face like threads of spider web. She was sitting sideways on a white horse, like ladies in the olden days did. The baby was just a lump inside her coat. Rain dripped off the roof of the carousel and made it look like a giant-size crystal chandelier, except you don't get wooden horses on chandeliers.

We were gobsmacked to see the girl because not many people visit fun parks that don't work, especially when there's a war going on.

1

Permission not to have a friend

Skip was my running-away name. It seemed like a good name because of how I skipped school whenever I was doing a runner. I still liked it, even after I found out that's what you call the massive metal bins that demolition crews dump their rubbish in. A skip is somewhere you can shelter when there's nowhere else, and getting a new name is a bit like being born all over again. I hoped my new life would be better than the one I'd left behind.

It was easy, once I decided to go. I made a plan and I kept it in my head because everyone knows you should never write a plan down in case someone else finds it. Even though it was the last day of term, before the holidays, I still went to school. That was part of my plan. If I didn't turn up the teachers would ring my caseworker because they knew I'd run away before, only then I hadn't made a plan so it was easy for them to find me. I heard the other kids telling their friends what they were going to do after school and in the holidays. Some were going to the beach and others were going to stay with their grandmother or their aunty or someone else they were related to. I didn't tell anyone what I was going to do. That was part of my plan, too. I even had a strategy for an unlikely event. If someone asked me over to their place after school, that would be an unlikely event because people only ask you to their house if they're your friend. But if anyone did, my strategy was to pretend not to hear.

Sometimes I made up reasons to myself why I had no friends. They were a bit like the notes some kids take to school so they don't have to play sport because of their sore knee or some other part of them that doesn't work properly. These are some of my reasons:

Dear Mr Kavanagh, Skip can't have a friend because he's moved to seven schools in three years and there's no time for him to get to know anyone properly.

Dear Mr Kavanagh, Skip can't have a friend in case he accidentally tells them something he's not supposed to.

Dear Mr Kavanagh, Skip can't have a friend in case they ask him about the bruises.

Dear Mr Kavanagh, Skip can't have a friend because he doesn't have a proper family to talk about.

Dear Mr Kavanagh, Skip can't have a friend because sometimes he doesn't hear people talking to him when he's drawing, and that makes them think he's rude or crazy.

Dear Mr Kavanagh, Skip can't have a friend because he's no good at maths, and they might think he's dumb.

As well as my excuses for not having friends I also invented other notes I'd like to take to school if only there was someone who'd write them for me.

Dear Mr Kavanagh, I give my permission for Skip to put his hands up to the sky because that's how he finds out about the light. It's important for him to see where it falls on his fingers and where the shadows begin and end, and the difference between sharp black shadows and soft grey ones.

Dear Mr Kavanagh, I give my permission for Skip to look out the window whenever he wants and for as long as he wants because he's not being lazy, he's thinking about important things like colour and light.

Dear Mr Kavanagh, I give my permission for Skip to spend every day making pictures or looking at other people's pictures because that's how he makes sense of the world.

Dear Mr Kavanagh, Please don't punish Skip for drawing, even if he's doing it when you think he should be doing maths.

I hoped that where I was going I wouldn't have to explain myself to anyone.

The night before I ran away I got Dad's coat out of the toolshed, where I'd hid it, and stuffed it in my backpack. It still stunk of smoke, and the blackened bits around the hem crumbled in my hands like burnt toast. I left early the next morning, so no one would ask awkward questions about my bulging bag. School finished at two o'clock on the last day of term, so there was no one from my pretend family waiting to pick me up. I filled my pockets with chalk, and walked to the station. I bought a ticket to the city with money I'd found under the sofa cushions. The train was waiting. It was midnight-blue, my favourite colour for trains, and I stepped onto it before I had time to change my mind. When the doors closed behind me I felt like a bird had got inside my chest and was beating its wings trying to get loose, and it wasn't leaving much room for me to breathe.

At Central Station I got off. I went to the toilets and put Dad's coat on, even though there was nearly a heatwave. It was all I had left of him, except what was inside my head. The counsellor told me there had to be give and take if I was going to settle with my new foster family. She said that Mrs Ransome was probably only trying to help me move on when she tried to burn Dad's coat.

When I came out of the cubicle I stood side-on so I could only see the left side of my face in the mirror. That's the side of me that looks brave, thinks brave and acts brave; the side that says I don't need friends or family. It's my chestnut side. Once, my dad said that God was a woman and She couldn't make up her mind what colour eyes She liked best, chestnut-brown or pigeon-grey, so She gave me one of each. I try not to look at things with my grey side because it reminds me of my dad, and I don't want to be like him. Pigeon-grey is like a shadow. It's not real by itself; something else has to be there for it to exist. That's how it was when my mother left: my dad started to disappear.

I stepped out into the subway and got swept along with a swarm of people all looking like they had places to go. Homes and families was my chestnut thought. Not all homes are happy, the grey whispered like a ghost. I hitched Dad's coat up and put one sneaker down on the metal teeth of the escalator, and then the other. It took me up to street level where God rays streamed down between the skyscrapers and made all kinds of interesting angles and shadows. I stopped and put my hands up to the sky, but it's hard to be still in a big city. People bump into you and look annoyed, as if stopping's against the law and looking at the light isn't normal. So I put my arms down and followed the others, but only as far as the mall.

I liked the mall right away. Banners stretched from one side to the other like smiles, the never-ending kind of smile you'd give your mother if she came back for you. People acted different in the mall. They walked slow if they felt like it. They looked in windows and sat on steps and fed their lunch crumbs to the birds. I spotted a bunch of people watching something and I edged in between them till I could see what they were looking at.

There were three people drawing on the pavement with chalk. There was an old black woman, a young guy with a barbed-wire tattoo around his throat and a man with wrinkles like canyons on his forehead. I figured he might be someone's dad, or maybe his wife had left him or else he'd been in a war sometime, because you don't get wrinkles on your forehead like that for no reason. The weirdest thing was that no one told the people drawing to scram, and no one spat on their pictures or peed on them. It was like a miracle. I knew I'd been right to come. I sat down on Dad's coat and watched. The pictures were good, really good. I'd never imagined proper artists using chalk. The only reason I did was because I could get stubs of it for free.

The black woman looked up at me. I couldn't tell what colour her eyes were. They were wet and dark and shining, like pools of deep, still water. For a second I thought I could see pictures in them, like I was looking right inside her to where her memories were. She smiled, and I wondered if she knew what I'd seen or if she could see the pictures I kept hidden inside myself. Then she went back to her drawing. She had long white hair and a necklace made of feathers, shells and string. The feathers were bright red and sky blue. I never saw feathers like that before. City birds are nearly always dull, except for the pigeons with their rhubarb toes and emerald-and-violet collars. I wondered where the black lady came from, and if she missed the birds.

I sat there for a long time, maybe hours. The old lady with the magic eyes left but I was still there when the two guys wrapped their chalks up in scraps of rag and slapped the rainbow-coloured dust out of their pants. After they'd gone I took a closer look at the pictures. An old man was looking too. I'd seen him before, in the crowd. It was Billy, but I didn't know him then.

There was a picture of an American Indian wearing a feathered headdress. It was drawn to fit inside an oval shape, and the colours were orangey-brown and white, like a really old photo. You could tell the guy who drew it knew all about light and shade because of the wrinkles on the Indian's face. It looked like you could stick your fingers in them. Beside the Indian picture was another oval with writing in it. Together, the two ovals looked like one of those lockets girls hang around their neck, only this one was much bigger.

The old man, who was Billy, said, 'It's s'posed to be Chief Seattle. He's famous for some speech he made over a hundred and fifty years back. Said some pretty important things that people have remembered ever since. That's a bit of his speech.' He nodded towards the words inside the oval.

My mother's photo also fits inside a locket. I wished I could remember if she said any important things to me, so I could write them in the oval opposite her picture. I know it's not a hundred and fifty years since I saw Mum, but it sure seems like a long time. They told me I was nearly twelve, but sometimes it felt like I'd been around a lot longer. Maybe they lied about my age; they told me other things that weren't true. All I knew for sure was that I was somewhere between being born and being dead.

I wished I could draw my mother on the pavement, next to Chief Seattle, but I can't remember her face. Her photo was taken from far away. She was standing in a backyard, next to a clothes line and in front of a shed, and she was holding something small, wrapped in a blanket. I can't see what's inside the blanket but I know it's me. The person who took the photograph didn't know that shadows are as important as light. We need both of them to help us see things the way they really are. In the photo of my mother there aren't any shadows, and I can't see her face for the light.

The drawing next to Chief Seattle was done mostly in red and black. These are the colours of war. Once I saw a war on television, but my dad threw a chair at it and sparks and smoke and a terrible stink came out. It was like the war had really been there, inside the television. We didn't have a television after that.

Billy said the name of the war picture was Armageddon. There was a diagonal red stripe across it, the way the council does when something is banned, like dogs or skateboards. I think the artist wanted war banned, which is a good idea because wars kill a lot more people than dogs do and I don't think skateboards have killed anyone at all yet.

2

Vincent and the wedding birds

Billy and me looked at the pictures until it started getting dark. 'You hungry?' he said.

I'd saved my lunch: two cheese and Vegemite sandwiches and an apple, just like in the plan. I followed Billy down a flight of stairs to a food court and we sat outside Sam's Kebabs and shared my sandwiches. I put Dad's coat on again because I saw Billy looking at the bruises on my arms, but he didn't ask me about them. We didn't talk much at all. We just watched Sam's fifty-two-centimetre flat-screen television and tried to lip-read because we couldn't hear the sound.

Sam turned his TV off after the late news and Billy got up and walked away. When I was making my plan I'd never worried about a place to sleep. The most important thing was to make my getaway. But now it was dark I wasn't so sure. I followed Billy up the stairs. He turned around when he got to the top and I thought he was going to say something. I was waiting for him to tell me to get lost, but he didn't. He just disappeared himself around the corner.

I waited a bit and then bolted up the stairs and watched him shuffling along the street. He walked lopsided, like one leg was shorter than the other. When he was nearly a block away I started walking slowly after him, hoping he'd lead me to a safe place to sleep. He crossed the road but by the time I got there the traffic lights had turned red. A whole bunch of people dressed in fancy clothes poured out of a building onto the footpath just as Billy walked by. I fixed my eyes on him so I wouldn't lose sight of him. Then I felt an arm go around my shoulders. I had to take my eyes off Billy to look sideways at the face pressed too close to mine. I saw black stubble poking through mud-coloured make-up, electric-blue eyelids and lips as red as parrot feathers. I felt sick.

'Need a bed for the night, sweetheart?' Hot breath filled my ear and that bird got inside me again, flapping and flapping against my rib cage.

'I'm . . . I'm with him!' I said, pointing across the road. 'Billy, wait up Billy!' I yelled.

He turned around and I stepped out on the road. Horns blared and tyres squealed as I dodged and weaved between the cars. I made it to the safety island and then the lights changed and I darted across to the other side. Once Billy saw I was okay he walked off like nothing had happened.

'You can't come where I'm goin', kid,' he said over his shoulder.

'Why not?'

'It's a refuge for blokes.'

'I'm a bloke.'

'No you're not, you're a kid.'

'How old would I have to be to get in?'

'Eighteen, and if you're going to tell me you're nearly eighteen, don't bother.'

'It doesn't make sense,' I said.

'What doesn't?'

'They'll let you stay if you're a man but they won't if you're a kid.'

'Doesn't have to make sense,' said Billy. 'They've got rules and the rules are all that count.'

'What sort of rules?'

'Rules about everything. There's lists of them stuck up on the walls like the Ten bloomin' Commandments.'

It was on the tip of my tongue to ask what the Ten Commandments were when Billy said, 'And number one commandment is: Thou shalt not ask too many questions.'

Then he stopped so suddenly I almost bumped into him. He spun around and grabbed me by the shoulders. 'Listen kid, if I let you in here and you get sprung, the Welfare will be around to pick you up before you can blink. So you'd better make yourself scarce if you don't want to end up back where you came from.'

For a couple of seconds I thought he might be telling the truth. But it didn't take me long to figure out he was only worried he might get kicked out if he let me stay. I was used to people not wanting me around. I don't know why I thought Billy might be different.

To our left was an old two-storey building. It was made of grey stone and had bars on the windows. A fence of metal spikes guarded the building and each one had a little arrow on top like a devil's pitchfork. I watched Billy do something to a panel on the fence and then the gate opened and he limped past the pitchforks and disappeared himself into the bushes beside the building. I didn't know if he left the gate open on purpose. I just made sure no one was watching before I walked through. Some of the blinds on the downstairs windows weren't pulled right down and enough light leaked out for me to see a path. I followed it around the back of the building until I came to a small separate room with a wooden door and no windows. I felt for a switch, before I nipped inside, closed the door and turned the light on.

There was a sink up one end and a broken toilet at the other, full of black water. Spider webs clung to the walls and ceiling. The floor was covered with used paper towels, dead leaves and other more disgusting things. I wondered about going someplace else but when I saw the lock on the door and remembered the lady-man at the traffic lights I spread Dad's coat over everything and lay down. It stunk in there, so I jammed my face next to the gap under the door and breathed in silver and black, the smell of night. I promised myself I'd find a better place in the morning.

I didn't think anyone would be looking for me – they were probably glad I'd gone – but for the first two weeks I never slept in the same place twice in a row, just in case. It was hard to fall asleep some nights. There's a lot of reasons why a person can't go to sleep. Being hungry is one reason, or because of the places where they have to sleep, like under railway bridges or in builders' skips. Sometimes I didn't want to go to sleep in case I dreamt about lady-men with electric-blue eyelids. Other times I slept in the daytime, when there were plenty of people around, so I could stay awake at night. Running away was easy; not knowing what to do next was the hard part.

I didn't know if I'd ever see Billy again after that first day, because the city was so big and there were so many people. But I saw him often. I learnt to know the places I'd find him. Sometimes at Sam's Kebabs, sometimes at the mall, watching people draw, and sometimes on the steps of St Mary's. The first time I saw him, I sat close by, but I never talked to him. I thought he might still be mad at me for following him to the refuge. The next day I handed him half a pie I'd found in a bus shelter. He ate it but didn't say anything. After that I used to go and sit with him whenever I saw him. Sometimes we'd talk and sometimes not, but I never asked him any questions in case I made him mad again.

One day, about a month after I'd run away, I was headed down to the river to watch the boats. I heard the bells of St Mary's ringing and I knew it must be six o'clock. That was dinner time at the refuge. I figured I wasn't going to see Billy that day, although I'd looked in all the regular places. But when I got to the grass beside the water, Billy was sitting there at one of the tables. I'd got close enough to see the bandage before he saw me. Then he looked up and pulled his hand out of sight under the table. We watched the boats and talked until the lights came on in the cafes behind us. All that time Billy looked straight ahead and I never asked him about his bandaged hand.

'I'm hungry,' I said. 'I gotta go. I found a place you can get bread for free. They leave their leftovers in a laneway, garbage bags full of it. But you've gotta get there before the charity people do or they take the lot.'

I didn't look back. I knew Billy would come with me if he wanted to eat. I heard him shuffling after me and smiled a bit. I didn't see his face till we were waiting to cross the road. He had to turn his head to see the traffic. He could only see out of his right eye. The left side of his face was smashed. You couldn't even tell if his eye was still there. Everything was swollen up like a rotten fish. I looked away fast. I thought I was going to spew in the gutter.

We got cheese rolls and Danishes and went under the bridge to eat them. I had the apple Danish and I gave Billy the blueberry because they're the best ones you can get. Billy took a long time to eat. After he was finished he said, 'Thought I might rough it while the weather's good.'

Sometimes, if you waited long enough, Billy told you the answer before you asked the question. 'I've moved out of the refuge,' he said. 'There was a bit of an incident.'

I tried not to be too pleased that Billy was going to hang out with me. I reminded myself he was probably only there because he'd been in a fight and they'd kicked him out. It wasn't as if I was the reason he'd left.

When he found out I had trouble sleeping, Billy taught me about *visualisation*. He said it was a useful technique to use when you found yourself in *difficult circumstances*. Turns out, visualisation is what I do when I'm making pictures. I imagine things in my head and draw them, except I can't imagine my mother's face. When I'm trying to go to sleep, I like to picture some place I've been to in real life, or something that's really happened to me. Billy said it's okay to do that or you can make something up if you want to, like being on a tropical island. The thing I like to visualise best of all, especially when it's cold, happened one hot night when I drew the wedding birds.

It was on the Friday before pension day, almost three months after Billy and I met. Billy had no money and I was nearly out of chalk, so we pinched six packets from the Reject Shop. When we found out they were all white, I had the idea about seagulls. I wanted to draw a gigantic flock of them on the footpath outside St Mary's

Cathedral. There were always weddings there on Saturdays, and I wanted to make it look like my chalk birds were eating the rice that people threw at the bride and groom. Billy says throwing rice is supposed to bring good luck but I don't know why, unless the people getting married haven't got anything to eat.

We stayed up till two o'clock in the morning. Billy kept a lookout in case the police came while I was drawing. I don't think the police like art being done on footpaths. I was nearly finished. I used the last bit of my black to give the birds their shadows, and I had a stub of red left to draw legs on the ones that were standing in the gutter. Then I heard the footpath-sweeping machine. It came out of a laneway one block up, did a left-hand turn and was whizzing down our side of the street. Billy and me disappeared ourselves into the shadows beside the church.

All the sweepers had a sign on them that said: 'Caution, slow moving vehicle'. During the day that was true, but at night-time the drivers cut loose. I thought this one was going to run over my seagulls for sure, but he didn't. He stopped and got out and squatted on the heels of his boots to take a closer look. Billy stepped out then and I heard the driver say, 'They're bloody unreal, mate. No kidding, I half expected 'em to fly away when I got close!'

Billy turned around and signalled with his head and I knew it was okay to come out.

'This is Skip,' he said. He never called me 'kid' any more. 'Skip drew the birds. He's going to be a famous artist one day.'

'Another Leonardo, mate?' the driver said.

'Could be,' answered Billy, nodding.

'Archimedes,' said the driver, sticking out his hand, 'Call me Archie.'

He and Billy shook hands and then they sat down on the seat outside St Mary's. Archie took a cigarette from behind his ear like he was a magician and he and Billy shared it as if they were old friends.

They talked about my picture for a while and then Archie said, 'I reckon my old man could've been an artist, except he was a mollydooker. Back in them days the teachers used to give kids the cuts for drawing or writing with their left hand. So me old man gave up drawing. But later on, when he got crook and couldn't work, he used to design stuff for a bloke who does tattoos. This is one of his.'

Archie lifted up his high-visibility shirt and pointed to a tattoo of a leopard. It was really beautiful, even though it had tufts of black chest hair growing out of its back. When Archie flexed his muscles it looked like the leopard was going to leap off his chest.

After that, he and Billy talked about pigeon poo on public buildings and the Grand Prix, which is a car race, while I finished off my wedding birds. I wondered if Archie was a racing car driver in his spare time because of the way he drove the footpath-sweeper.

After Archimedes left, Billy and me went under the bridge near the station to sleep. At night you can't tell the river's muddy, and even though the sky is too full of light to see the stars you can see the city reflected in the water. It looks a bit like a painting Vincent van Gogh did before he cut off his ear. It's called *Starry Night over the Rhône River*. It isn't his most famous picture but it's still my favourite. If I painted something as beautiful as that I'd never try to cut my ear off. *Starry Night over the Rhône River* makes me feel peaceful. On the hot night in March when I drew the wedding birds, I went to sleep trying to remember how many stars Vincent had painted in the sky. That's the bit I visualise over and over again: Billy and me lying on the river bank, looking up at the sky. I hear water slapping against boats and I smell mud and water and hamburgers.

One day I'll make a plan and go to France. I'll go at night and lie on my back and look up at the stars Vincent looked at. Maybe they'll be the same stars Chief Seattle saw, only he was over in America. Anyway, I'll look at them with both eyes at the same time because then I won't be nearly twelve years old and I'll know exactly who I'm supposed to be.

3

Overcoats and irises

Sometimes I like to work things out backwards, from the end to the beginning. Like how come I wasn't in the Queen's Elbows on that freezing winter night in July. I'll bet if you did a survey, most people would say it was because I was sleeping in the skip on the demolition site that used to be a hospital. But that was only the last thing. It's a bit like when you ask someone where they come from and they tell you what suburb they live in, but if they kept on going backwards they would end up inside their mother's belly or maybe even somewhere before that, like in the ocean or deep space or in God's mind. I think this means that everyone really comes from the same place. People who believe in reincarnation could just keep on going backwards for infinity.

When I was backwards thinking about the third of July, I only got as far as Michaela. She's not in this story much, but she's the reason why some of the things happened. And besides, I want to tell you about her because, if I don't, no one else might. It's possible that Billy and Max and me are the only ones left who knew her.

When Billy found out I was interested in art he started taking me to the State Library. I didn't think we'd be allowed inside, but Billy said the library belonged to the people and we were the people. He said even if you didn't have a coat you could still go there, as long as your hands were clean. That was in the rules, he said, and he could prove it because someone wrote them down when they first built the library. It was warm in there and it was free, and Billy showed me where to find Ned Kelly's original armour and a book worth twelve million dollars. But the best things were the books about art.

That's how we knew Michaela, because she worked at the library and wore a badge with her name on it. Michaela was beautiful. Her legs were way long, which must have come in handy for reaching books on high-up shelves. Her hair was cut short and spiked like boys' hair. It was the colour of autumn leaves and it wasn't fake colour, either, because the hairs on her arms were the same. The freckles on Michaela's nose and cheeks looked like the flecks of colour Monet painted on pictures of his lily pond, to represent sunlight, and she wore seven studs in one ear and none in the other. I liked that because I like odd things. I think it's because of my eyes. Michaela's eyes were both the same. They were the colour of the irises in Monet's garden.

I don't know if Michaela had any kids. She looked old enough to be married but she didn't wear any rings on her fingers. Sometimes I wondered what it would be like if she took me home to her place to live. I imagined she'd have a lot of books at her house and she'd be kind. But I knew it was stupid to imagine things like that, especially after she spotted me outside the soup kitchen at the Queen's Elbows.

I was soaking up warmth from the red-brick wall behind me, with half a bread roll stuffed in my cheek and my hands wrapped around a mug of Salvation Soup that tasted exactly like Vegemite with hot water in it and looked like the vinyl on the floor in the toilets at McDonald's. Most people don't look at you when you're in a soup queue; not really look. I think they're scared to. But Michaela wasn't scared. She did a double take and our eyes met and her mouth opened like goldfish lips, only pink, and I thought she was going to say something. It was me who looked away first.

I thought she might be a do-gooder, and Billy had warned me about them. He said they were kind and well meaning but they didn't always understand the *complexities*. Billy knows a lot of words. He believes in improving yourself. That's another reason why he used to take me to the library. He also reckons the best way to understand something is to find it out for yourself. I found out what complexities are because of something that happened when Billy and me were looking for somewhere to stay at the end of June.

Billy had to sleep inside when it was winter, on account of his arthritis. He got a bed in a place that used to be a pub. They turned it into a refuge and called it Hope House, but nearly everyone still called it the Queen's Elbows. After he got his place sorted out Billy said he'd help me find somewhere to stay. I was a bit surprised; I didn't think he'd bother about me, even though he hardly ever got mad with me any more.

We found a hostel for women and children and Billy asked the person in charge if I could stay, but she said I'd have to be accompanied by an adult. Billy said he'd accompany me, but she told him he couldn't come in there because it was only for women and children. I never had a woman look after me, except in the beginning when my mother was there, but I don't remember that. And the ones who came after her don't count because they didn't look after me. I had Dad and then I had Billy. I couldn't figure out why I needed a woman to get into that place or why they didn't let kids in the men's shelter if they were accompanied by an adult.

This was a complexity. Complexities are like maths, I thought, and I'm dumb at both. The woman started asking questions. I got worried because Billy's fists kept bunching up like he wanted to punch her lights out. His eye was nearly better and I didn't want him getting in any more incidents. I touched his sleeve and he looked down at me and for a minute I thought I'd done the wrong thing. But then he took me by the hand and we walked back to the men's place in the rain. No one had ever held my hand before except for Dad. I was surprised you can be as old as me and holding hands still feels okay. I wondered if Billy was like Dad but I didn't want him to be because my father was a damaged man.

Every night for three weeks I hid in the laundry of the Queen's Elbows, but I hardly slept at all. I was scared someone would find me and Billy would get kicked out again. Then Michaela saw me in the soup queue and I knew I had to go back to sleeping rough in case she was one of those kind, well-meaning do-gooders that Billy told me about.

I put Dad's overcoat on before I wrapped myself up like a Christmas present in pink-and-silver builders' foil. I was glad the kids at my last school couldn't see, but it didn't matter to me about the colours. Sometimes clouds are pink and so are watermelons and babies' lips, and anyway, you can see on a colour wheel that pink's just red with white mixed in with it. I lay there in the skip for a while, looking out at the slice of neon sky. I hardly noticed the broken bricks digging into me because I kept thinking about never being able to go back to the State Library. I was trying to figure out some way around it when I heard Billy coming.

I knew it was him because of the sound of his bad leg dragging on the footpath. In winter the cold got in his bones and made it worse. That's why he nearly always had odd shoes on, because one wore out before the other. When he got another pair from the op shop he used to donate the one he didn't need. He usually put it in a charity bin outside, but one day he gave it to the op shop lady and she said she couldn't accept a single shoe until Billy told her there might be someone else out there who had a bad leg like him, except on the other side. She hadn't thought of that, so she took the shoe and said, 'God bless you, sir.' This was another complexity because I couldn't work out if Billy was being funny or kind, although he is both, but not always at the same time.

I unwrapped myself from the foil and got out of the skip because it was hard for Billy to climb in when his leg was playing up. I told him about Michaela. I had to because he wanted me to go back to the shelter with him.

'Do you think she's a do-gooder?'

'Dunno, Skip,' he said. 'She looks like she'd have a soft heart, but that's the problem. They're usually the ones who want to help and they just don't know the right way to go about it.'

Then I said the thing that worried me the most: 'I can't go back to the library then.' It wasn't a question so Billy didn't have to answer, but I wanted him to say something. Something good.

'You've got a gift; make the most of it, Skip,' he said. 'You gotta get an education and do something worthwhile with your life.'

I didn't know how I was going to do all this stuff if I couldn't go back to the library. I closed my fingers around the packet of chalks in my pocket and squeezed my eyelids shut. What Billy said was like something my dad would have said. But saying stuff, even if it's good, isn't enough. Dad never did anything, he just talked about it. Even I knew you needed plans.

After Billy went back to the Queen's Elbows I climbed into the skip again and wrapped myself up. Then I started thinking about overcoats. That's another thing I do sometimes when I'm trying not to think about stuff that's happened or might happen or might not. This is what I know so far:

The word coat makes people think about feelings like comfort, warmth, friendship, safety and happiness.

Using an object this way when you write is called *symbolism*.

In real life, coats can be used to cover up things no one wants to know about: ugly stuff like bruises and half-smoked cigarettes you've picked up off the footpath to swap for something to eat. And stolen chalk.

Some people think you can use a coat, like a fake smile, to cover up invisible things like a broken heart or hate or being afraid. (If you have some or all of these things they say you are *damaged*.)

People who have invisible damage to hide sometimes wear khaki coats with metals buttons and medals on them.

My dad had a coat like that and so did Billy. (The young soldier at the Carousel of War and Peace had one too, but I didn't know about him then.)

Sometimes the best disguise is not wearing a coat, so people think you have nothing to hide.

Number seven was why I decided to stop wearing Dad's coat to the State Library. Billy and me had made a plan to go back there in the morning and I didn't want to give Michaela another reason to think I was homeless.

The next day was Pension-day Thursday. That day only came around once a fortnight, and it was when Billy bought me new chalks. I stuffed Dad's overcoat in my backpack and cleaned myself up in the McDonald's rest rooms before I met Billy. Then we bought chalk for me and cigarettes for him before we went to the library to carry out the plan. As soon as we got inside Billy went over to Michaela and asked her where to find the art books, even though we both knew exactly where they were.

'It's for my grandson, Skip,' Billy said and he winked at me with the eye that wasn't next to Michaela. 'He's visiting from interstate while his family's away on business. He's an art student and he's studying the Masters.'

'I've seen your art on the footpath,' Michaela said, and she was smiling. 'I like it very much.'

That was the first time she ever spoke to me, and I couldn't think of a single word to say back. I followed her and Billy to the art section, and I kept thinking about how she called my chalk drawings 'art' and how Billy pretended I was his grandson. I thought that was a stroke of genius because it wasn't even part of the plan.

We spent all morning at the library and I felt different. It wasn't just because I didn't have Dad's coat on. I felt safe, like I really did have a grandpa. When we went outside we sat on the steps. Billy opened his packet of cigarettes and I opened my new box of chalks and took out the blue and the green. I already knew what I was going to draw. I'd looked at the picture every time I came to the library and now I thought I knew it by heart. By the time I'd finished, the blue and the green were worn down to stubs but it was worth it.

I did a pond, like the one in Monet's famous garden. I even drew pebbles on the bottom because in real life Monet made sure the water in his pond was so clear he could see the light reflected in it. And I drew waterlilies floating on top, and touches of white and yellow to show the light, the way Monet did, only his touches were paint and mine were chalk. I really like the way Monet did hundreds of tiny brushstrokes that look a bit blurry close up, then when you step back it all becomes clear. It's a little bit like the 3D Magic Eye pictures they used to print in the newspaper on Saturdays, where you have to put the paper right up close to your eyes and then gradually move it further and further away until all of a sudden you can see something you couldn't see before and it's like you stepped right inside another world.

Sometimes I wonder if life is like that. I wonder if God is up there, standing back like Monet from his easel, and He or She can make sense of all the stuff that happens on earth: war and violence and everything. Or maybe God is like me, with different coloured eyes, and things are beautiful and happy, or sad and ugly, depending on which eye He closes and which one He leaves open. Michaela was beautiful whichever eye I looked out of, and even when I looked with both.

When I finished my pond Billy said, 'Makes me want to take my boots off and dip my feet in, Skip.'

Billy never washed his feet in winter. He said it was bad for you because it stripped all the natural oils from your skin and let the chill seep up through your feet into your body. But I knew he was giving me a compliment about my drawing.

After a while I noticed people were walking around my pond instead of across it. Billy noticed too. I remember the smile on his face. I wished Michaela would come out and have her lunch on the grass like she sometimes did. I wanted her to look into Monet's pond with her iris-coloured eyes. But even though the sun was shining and the sky was pure blue, the air was cold because it was July, and Michaela didn't come out. I didn't know I would never see her again.

4

Red and black

Red is brave, happy, loud and fast, and sometimes dangerous or angry. Black is soft, slow, silent and sad, but it can be angry, too. I know this because of the words chalked on the footpath next to Chief Seattle:

'When our young men grow angry at some real or imaginary wrong, and disfigure their faces with black paint, it denotes that their hearts are black.'

War is mostly black and red.

Bradley Clark thought everyone else was the devil when he had his fits. He tried to stab people with his potato peeler, and hurled furniture at the walls of the refuge. He was like a shattered stained-glass window: something beautiful that's broken; a million colours fallen on the ground where no light can get through.

When I woke up in the night after I'd drawn the lily pond there was no colour and no light. There was only sound. More sound than I'd ever heard in my life. Enough to make my eardrums bleed. My eyes, nose and mouth were full of dust. No room for air, no breath to scream for help and no way anyone could have heard. My body hurtled out of control. I was a star falling into a black hole. I was Bradley Clark, possessed by the devil, inside a concrete mixer or an earthquake, going mad. I was a damaged person. And then something clicked in my brain and I knew I was in the skip. I had to get out, dodge bricks, broken concrete, cover my head, find the lid and breathe. My lungs were about to explode when the skip slammed hard into something and stopped. The lid peeled back as easy as a note off a sticky pad. The skip was on its side. Rubbish spewed out on the street. I dragged a mixture of dust and air down my windpipe, pulled my legs free and crawled out into the red and the black.

The world was full of screaming: people, sirens, alarms and machines. Fires burnt everywhere. The skyline was a bleeding mouth of broken teeth.

I ran and ran, looking for a place I knew, a face I knew; looking for Billy. I dodged massive concrete columns flung across the streets like pick-up sticks, ran past stairways going nowhere, windows with no glass, piles of steel spaghetti and water gushing metres high from broken pipes. I saw lanes of cars crushed flat, like softdrink cans, with their drivers still inside them. I threw up beside an upside down bus. Its windows were filled with squashed faces and staring eyes that didn't see me. My sneakers stuck to the dark stains that leaked out on the footpath, and I ran again. Clouds of dust and smoke and darkness made it hard to find my way.

'Billy! Billy!' I screamed, thinking I'd never find him because I didn't even know where I was. Then I saw a huge, stained-glass window. There was no building, not even a wall, just the window with a fire burning somewhere behind. It was a miracle. I thought that window might be the last beautiful thing left on earth, so I scrambled over the rubble and stood in front of it. The crimson and the amber fell across my bleeding arms. The man in the glass had blood on his head and his hands and on his pure, white robe. He had a long beard, and for a second I thought he might be a terrorist, but then I noticed he was holding a lamb and a curly walking stick, not a gun.

Behind me, a building erupted like a volcano, spewing red-hot lava into the streets. I turned to run again and saw the church spire of St Mary's, only it wasn't where it used to be. It was lying across the footpath and in the gutter where my wedding birds had been. The bells had buried themselves in concrete, and if you didn't know anything about concrete you'd think it was soft as butter. Because of St Mary's, I knew which way to go to find Billy.

A rhyme pounded against the inside of my head in time with my footsteps: 'Here's the church and here's the steeple, open the door and you'll see all the people.' Words from way back, when I was a little kid, when I had a father, before he let the ghosts get him. I played them over and over, like a scratched CD, to block out the black and the red: the bodies, the blood, the fire, the smoke, the hate, the anger and the damage. What had happened could only be war, and I knew all about what war did to people.

I tried to outrun the planes. My throat was raw. Every breath burnt like a blowtorch. When I got to the Queen's Elbows only the front wall was standing. Behind it was a pile of rubble big enough to fill thousands of skips. I bit my teeth together, hard, so there was no space for that flapping bird to get in. Billy's room was in the basement. I got down on my knees and shovelled away the rubbish with my hands until I found the grate where they used to roll beer barrels down to the cellar. I pulled a pitchfork off the fence and belted the rusty catch until it fell apart. Clinging to the edges, I lowered myself into the cellar until my freezing fingers gave way and I dropped down into the darkness. It felt like my leg bones had rammed through my shoulders. I lay on my back, hugging my legs, trying to stop the pain. Through the hole in the footpath I counted the planes – seven dark arrows against the gingerbread sky – and I wondered how much longer it would be until morning. But I couldn't wait until then; I had to find Billy.

I imagined Bradley Clark hiding with his potato peeler, thinking I was the devil. I shivered, but sweat or blood, or both, dripped off my face. I had to find Billy's room. I stuck my hands out like a sleepwalker, feeling my way. My foot clipped something – a ladder, and it clattered to the floor. I froze. No one came. I felt my way to a door and tried the handle. It was locked, so I hurled myself against it like the police do, but the middle was already busted and I fell through into the corridor.

'Billy!' I was past caring who else might be there. 'Billy!' My voice bounced back like it couldn't escape. I crept forward.

A corridor is meant to be straight and narrow; that's how I visualised it. I didn't know that the chimney from the ground floor had fallen through to the basement and blocked the corridor. Luckily I was going so slow I didn't fall over, but there was nothing I could do except sit down and wait until morning.

Then it was easy: I climbed up and over the bricks, calling Billy's name. He'd showed me his room the day he moved in. It was the first on the left. The two beds against the wall, where Shorty Long and Irish Kelly usually slept, were empty. A massive steel beam had collapsed. There was plaster and concrete everywhere but I saw a space underneath it; a cave just big enough for a bed to fit; Billy's bed. Since Shorty and Irish were gone, I guessed Billy would have made it out too but I had to be sure. I crawled in on my hands and knees. Waterfalls of sand and plaster trickled between the cracks. Everything was covered in white, like it had been snowing. There was just enough light to show Billy's coat and the still shape of a body underneath. I couldn't see his head on the pillow, only blood and the fallen beam.

I crouched in the corner crying and sleeping. Time had no meaning. I only got up because there was something I wanted to do before it got too dark. I took Shorty's blanket and cleared dust away from around Billy's bed. Then I drew yellow flowers because yellow is the colour of happiness and that's what Billy made me feel. It's also the colour of kindness, and Billy was kind even though he pretended not to be. Next I did a white cross at the bottom and wrote 'RIP Billy'. Last, I drew a dog on the wall because Billy told me he used to have a dog once. It was a sausage dog called Pablo, after Picasso. Picasso painted a picture of a sausage dog on a plate. The dog's name was Lump. Lump and Picasso both died in 1973. Sometimes, if two people really love each other and one of them dies, the other one does too. I wonder if it's the same for dogs. I'd like to have a dog. I drew books for Billy, too, and a pair of glasses so he could read them when he got to wherever he was going. The books made me think of the State Library and Michaela and the smashed columns that looked like the ruins of ancient Rome.

It was hard to see inside the room by the time I finished drawing. I felt bad leaving Billy there by himself but I didn't think I could stay all night next to a dead person. I climbed back over the hill of bricks and into the storeroom where I could look out without being seen. I shifted the ladder underneath the hole in the footpath and stepped up a few rungs. The sky was still a dirty orange, as if earth had got stuck somewhere between day and night. Sirens howled like wild dogs, swarms of planes swooped, fast and low, and bullets bombarded anything left standing. The ladder started vibrating so I jumped down and watched from the shadows as twelve pairs of boots marched past. I was still trying to decide if it would be safer to stay where

I was or go somewhere else when a dark figure crouched beside the hole and I thought I heard my name, whispered like a question.

The ladder shook as a foot came down on the top step and then another. When a man stepped off the bottom rung and turned around I bolted, up over the hill of bricks and into Billy's room. I crawled back in next to the broken body on the bed and made myself as small as I could. Torchlight flashed across the walls where I'd drawn Billy's favourite things, then it fell on the yellow flowers and the white cross, and I felt it on my face, and the inside of my eyelids was dangerous red. Then the man's arms went around me and I knew he wasn't a ghost and I knew I wasn't damaged like my dad.

'It's Bradley Clark.' It was Billy's voice. 'He had one of his seizures, turned on someone, a new bloke who didn't know what was going on. He laid Brad out cold. I told them to put him on my bed till he came good. I loaned him my coat and left. I thought I'd bunk in with you for the night but I couldn't find you, Skip, I thought I'd lost you.'

Sometimes I can see colour without opening my eyes. I saw that Billy's heart was no colour and every colour. Like water or diamonds or crystals, it's pure and reflects the light.

5

Weapons of Max destruction

Billy and me took two grey blankets from the Queen's Elbows. We rolled them up and tied them tight with Bradley Clark's bootlaces. Then Billy shut his eyes and bowed his head and I saw him touch his fingers to his forehead and to his heart before he took back his overcoat that he had loaned to poor, dead Bradley.

I wondered what it would feel like to be Bradley Clark when he was alive. My dad told me once that there are worse things than being dead. I wondered if Bradley Clark ever wished he was dead. I rubbed out the 'Billy' under 'RIP' and wrote 'Bradley' instead, but I left the dog there because I heard that dogs are man's best friends and I don't think Bradley had any human friends.

After that, Billy and me climbed to the top of the bricks. The city was a sea below us. Pockets of light pooled in the dark like oil slicks. We were lost sailors with no stars above to guide us. I thought about Chief Seattle who said: 'The Indian's night is dark. Not a single star of hope hovers above his horizon.' And I wondered if Billy and me would ever see the stars again.

'They would have been aiming for Parliament House,' said Billy. 'Wars are all about politics.'

I didn't know much about war. I only knew I didn't want to talk about it or even think about it. Up until then I thought war only happened in other countries.

'Where are we going to sleep?'

Billy looked at me, but didn't answer.

'Let's find something to eat,' he said after a while.

Even when you haven't got arthritis in your hip, it's hard to walk across a heap of broken bricks. It's like waking up and finding there's a war on. Nothing's the way it used to be and it's difficult to get your balance. That's why I held Billy's hand.

We kept to arcades and alleyways, short-cutting and soft-stepping past intersections like black cats. Tanks crashed through the wreckage like giant armadillos. The city was like a movie set. There were fronts of buildings with nothing behind them. In some places, whole blocks were left standing while others were flattened. Billy warned me to keep away from the ones that were standing in case they fell, but I reckon he meant in case they got bombed. I didn't like going near the ones that were already down either; that's where you saw the most bodies and heard the awful moans and cries. I looked at Billy.

'Nothing you or me can do for them poor souls,' he said.

I knew he was right, but it still seemed wrong, just walking past. I concentrated on stepping over cracks in the concrete, and repeating words. Hit-and-miss, I said, hit-and-miss. They were poor shots, these soldiers. Hit-and-miss. They'd never hit all the tin ducks at the fun park; they'd never win a giant panda.

I saw the broken neon sign blinking on and off above the food court and remembered I hadn't eaten all day.

'Stay here,' whispered Billy and he limped down the blue, white and green tiled steps.

I didn't like him going without me. I stared at the black between the tiles and made my eyes go skinny so I could concentrate on the reverse pattern. A siren screamed close by. Lights smeared across the entry of the arcade: ribbons of dangerous red and ice-cold blue. Voices drifted up from the arcade. I listened for Billy's, but I couldn't hear him. Then he was there in the

flickering pinkish glow at the bottom of the stairs, signal-
ling for me to come down.

I guess there were about twenty people down there.
They were street people. I'd seen most of them before, at
free food places. They huddled around a pile of smashed
chairs they'd set on fire for warmth and light. The roller
doors on Sam's shop and all his neighbours' were locked.
The shiny, silver containers were empty, the warming
lights were off and the television screen was blank. I wondered where Sam was. Would he come back another day,
when all the mess was cleaned up?

The bins hadn't been emptied, but as usual there
weren't many leftovers in the one outside Sam's Kebabs.
Even the Chopstix bin didn't have much in it that night,
but I found a Number 51, which was lucky because that's
my favourite. It's lemon and honey chicken and there
was nearly half a large serve. A good thing about Chinese
leftovers is that they're in plastic containers. Billy doesn't
care about odds and evens. He had some Number 38,
which was pork in black bean sauce, and we shared some
special fried rice.

The people around the fire were talking about what
had happened and trying to figure out why and what they
were going to do. I didn't want to listen. I sat outside Sam's
place to eat. Billy was reading a newspaper. It was two days

old. I didn't mean to read the headlines but they were there, in bold black letters. I could see them afterwards, even with my eyes shut, as clear as if the words were stamped inside my eyelids: 'ARMED FORCES GEAR UP AS PEACE TALKS FAIL'. I got down from my seat. I needed to walk.

'Too much fried rice,' I told Billy.

As soon as we left the arcade, the sounds of war invaded my ears and I started making a list in my head to block them out. It was a list of the sounds I couldn't hear: buses, brakes, banging bin lids, buskers, bells and footpath sweepers. I was thinking about Archimedes when Billy grabbed me and pulled me into a doorway. A truck pulled out of a side street. The driver looked right at us. We stood still. He changed gears and drove around our corner, looking hard at Billy and me, then he pointed two fingers at us like he was aiming a gun. There were soldiers in the back with real guns but they didn't shoot us.

We watched the truck till it disappeared, then Billy said, 'Come on, let's find ourselves a place to stay.'

'Can we go to the library?'

'There won't be any heaters on, Skip,' Billy said.

'I know.'

'And Michaela won't be there.'

'I know.'

'She's probably home, somewhere out in the suburbs, safe and sound.'

I hoped what Billy said was true but I couldn't help wishing we'd see her again, just to make sure she was okay. I didn't tell him I'd seen the broken columns on the ground, in case he said we musn't go.

The library steps looked like a river of rocks, and only three columns were left out of the eight. The roof had caved in over the halls at the front of the building and the windows were smashed, but the dome over the reading hall looked okay which meant there must still be places inside where we could go. I was glad it was pretty dark and we couldn't see any dead people.

When we got inside the reading room there were a few lights on, but they were far apart and dim, like candles in a fog, and I kept blinking to make sure the people I could see weren't ghosts. Even the sound of their crying was ghostly. It was thin and high and made you wonder if you'd really heard it or just imagined it. Billy shone his torch around and I saw someone curled up under one of the tables. He wore a grey jacket and old-man pants with pleats, and a belt to hold them up. At first I thought he was dead, he was so still. Billy knelt down on the floor and rolled him over, like a slater, on his back. He was holding a book even though he was asleep. The book was big and his hands were small like the rest of him, and I saw that he was a little boy. The writing on the cover of his book was made from letters cut out of magazines and newspapers. It said: 'Max Montgomery's Book of After-school Activities'. The boy was wearing glasses, and when he opened his eyes they were big and round and shiny, like a possum's.

'Are you Max?' Billy said.

The boy sat up and stared at us for a while, like he was trying to decide if he should talk to us or not, and then he said, 'Yes. Has my mother sent you?'

'No,' said Billy. 'Are you expecting her to come?'

'Yes, and she said I mustn't go outside until she gets here.'

'How long have you been waiting?'

'I don't know,' said Max. 'Mummy's taking such a long time, so I had a nap. I woke up when I heard the noise and I thought it must be someone with weapons of Max destruction. People started screaming and pushing each other, trying to get outside to see what was happening, and other people were trying to get inside. I hid under the table. That's what you're supposed to do when there's an earthquake. Nobody told me what to do when someone's coming after you with weapons. Then the front of the library fell down and after that I did some more colouring in and waited under the table for Mummy until I fell asleep.'

'Best thing you could have done!' said Billy. 'Skip and me are going to have a nap soon.'

'We've got blankets,' I said.

'Have you got anything to eat?' asked Max.

Billy hung his torch from a chair so it shone down on us like a proper light. I hoped the batteries wouldn't go flat. Then he took something out of the pocket of his overcoat. It was wrapped in a Chopstix serviette. Slowly he unfolded it and the boy's mouth stayed open the whole time.

'Ta-da!' Billy said. A half-eaten banana fritter sat in the middle of the serviette. 'I was saving this for breakfast, but I suppose I could let you have a bit.'

I felt like smiling because Billy was being so kind and funny to Max and he never even met him before. It was the first time I felt like smiling since the day Billy pretended he was my grandpa and Michaela talked to me and I drew Monet's pond on the footpath, which was really only yesterday but seemed much longer.

'What is it?' Max asked.

'Never seen a banana fritter before?' Billy pretended he was shocked. Max shook his head. 'Well then, you're in for a treat.'

Max put down his book and nibbled away at the half-eaten fritter, and Billy got me to help him arrange some tables and chairs into a sort of cubbyhouse. We even put a roof on it.

'It's a bunker,' Billy said. 'We'll sleep in there.'

I guessed he was thinking we might get bombed in the night.

When I started to untie Bradley Clark's bootlaces, Max licked the sugar crystals off his fingers and said, 'I'm six now and I can tie my own shoelaces.'

We let him help us undo the knots but we didn't tell him the laces came out of a dead man's boots. When we finished we crawled inside the bunker and covered ourselves with the blankets; Billy and me with Max between us.

'I'll switch the torch off now, Max,' Billy said. 'Maybe when we wake up your mother will be here.'

Outside our bunker, people were still talking in their soft library voices, others were crying and some were snoring. From the foyer came the sound of chalky bricks shifting, clinking together as they tumbled. I wondered what the Prime Minister was doing. Was he lying in his bed thinking about the headlines and weapons of mass destruction, or how to get peace? Or maybe he was trying the visualisation technique to get to sleep. What if he was dead? Who would make up the rules about war and peace and other important things then?

Next I thought about the people flying around in planes with bombs in them, and the soldiers in the back of the truck, and I wondered why they didn't shoot Billy and me. Whose side were they on? Once, when I lived with my dad, some boys asked me to play with them at school. They were playing war and they asked me whose side I wanted to go on: the Americans or the Enemy. I said I wanted to go on the other side.

'Whady'a mean?' they said. 'There's only two sides: the Americans or the Enemy.'

'My dad says there's three sides.'

'Who's on the third side?'

'All the people who don't believe in war. Dad says there's more on the third side than the other two sides put together, but the ones on the third side don't have weapons.'

One of the boys yelled, 'Your dad's crazy, everyone knows that!'

From then on the boys never asked me to play anything with them.

6

A thief's prayer

When I woke up the next morning, it was like a dream come true. Billy and Max were asleep beside me and there were books all around us. I felt like there was a song inside me, even though there was a war going on outside. The feeling was a bit like when you're curled up in bed and the rain is bucketing down. But it was even more than that. Because of the war, I had Billy. Before that I knew he wouldn't stay. I was always thinking, tonight's going to be the last night, once his eye's better, once the warm weather comes, once he finds a place where they'll let me stay, he'll be gone. But now there was Max.

I squeezed out of the bunker, so I wouldn't wake the others. Light poured through the coloured glass in the high-up windows. The dome looked like a giant bicycle wheel with cellophane woven in and out of the spokes. I held my hands up, and green and pink light got all over my skin. Then I did a bad thing. I shut my eyes and prayed to God that Max's mother wouldn't come to the library for him. Max was only six years old. I was sure Billy wouldn't go away and leave him.

Other people in the library were waking up. Some of them never went to sleep in the first place. I heard them talking in the night; about what had happened, what they saw, who they'd lost, where they were going, where the tanks were and what to do next. Twenty-four hours after the first strike they were saying the same things.

The others weren't street people, like Billy and me; you could tell by their clothes. Two days ago, people with nice clothes and shining hair wouldn't have looked at you, except for Michaela and the Salvos. Sometimes you might catch a stranger's quick sideways look that tripped your heart up and then it would be gone faster than a falling star, making you wonder if you'd only imagined it. But that morning, people looked long and slow at strangers' faces. I used to look at faces that way. I thought that maybe if I looked hard enough and long enough I'd find the person I was looking for. I imagined that if I saw my mother I'd know her, even though I can't remember what she looked like. And anyway, if I didn't, I was sure she'd know me because of my eyes.

When Max woke up I saw him looking for his mother and I tried not to think about what I'd asked God. The only person I looked for in the library was Michaela, but she wasn't there.

Billy followed Max out of the bunker. 'We'll have to find something to eat,' he said. 'C'mon, the sooner we go the sooner you'll get fed.' But Max wouldn't go outside because of his mother telling him not to. 'Well, you stay here with Max, Skip, and I'll go and get food.'

I wished Max would come along, so we could all go, but then I thought about what the boys at school said: that people on the third side got shot at by both the other sides.

Billy limped through a jagged hole in the wall and crossed the lawn where Michaela sometimes ate her lunch. He left his trademark tracks in the dewy grass: a perfect footprint on one side and a half-moon on the other.

Not so long after Billy left the library, it seemed like a lot of other people had gone too, but I didn't see where they went. The ones left in the reading room all looked old. One lady was knitting, some were reading, others just sat there hunched up, staring out through the smashed windows at the smoke and broken buildings. The sound of tumbling bricks that I'd heard the night before started up again. After a while I figured out it was coming from the foyer, so when Max got back in the bunker to find his Book of After-school Activities, I went to see what was making the noise. I discovered that's where some of the other people had gone. With scraps of rag tied over their noses and mouths, they climbed the rubble, shifting smaller pieces of brick and concrete with their hands and levering huge chunks out with pieces of pipe or timber. Suddenly I knew what they were trying to do. I raced back to the reading room and Max.

'Where were you?' he said.

'Do you want to go upstairs and look at the high-up books?' My legs were shaking.

'No, I'm going to do some cutting and pasting.'

I knew he wanted to be there to see his mother, but I didn't want him to see her if she was under the bricks in the foyer. And if she was, I felt like it would be my fault. Maybe I'd get sent to hell for the prayer I'd said.

Max opened his book and the small wooden box with the sliding lid where he kept his crayons, his coloured pencils, his glue stick and his blunt scissors. He mostly drew animals with big teeth and bellybuttons. I wished he could have seen the leopard on Archimedes' chest, so he'd have a better idea of muscles.

I got a dictionary and looked up 'max', and I found out it's short for 'maximum'. Then I looked up 'maximum' and it said: 'the greatest possible number, amount or intensity'. This means that if someone has weapons of max destruction they have weapons that can cause the greatest possible destruction, like bombs. Max had been right and he didn't even know it.

Billy was taking forever. I went and stood with a bunch of other people where there used to be a wall. We all stared out between the splintered planks and plastic-coated electrical wires; the bones and arteries of the library. The city was a rubbish dump. Machines crawled over it like scavenging rats. From where we were, they sounded like blowflies. Compared to what the city was like before, it was deserted, but there were still some people wandering around, watching the machines, dodging the army jeeps that prowled the streets, and ducking for cover when they heard the planes getting close.

I wondered if I'd been wrong to think Billy would stay because of Max. After a while, a lady with drawn-on eyebrows came by with a king-size coffee tin. She took the lid off and let me choose a biscuit.

'Are you waiting for your father?' she said.

'I haven't got a father.'

'My mother will be coming soon,' said Max. 'I think she might have gone shopping.'

It was like he couldn't see or hear what was going on outside. The lady held out the tin to him and stroked his hair with her grandma hands, and the only part of her face that looked happy was her beautiful bird's-wing eyebrows. 'Take another biscuit to keep you going,' she said.

Suddenly the people by the wall rushed back into the room like a wave on a beach. 'Keep back!' they said, but I wanted to look. A black van crept up the hilly street towards us. Even the windows were black. Weaving in and out to miss flattened cars and smashed columns, it climbed the jumbled stone steps and stopped where the foyer used to be. The tumbling noises in the foyer stopped. The driver jumped out and rushed around to the back of the van and I catapulted myself across the room.

'Come on, Max!'

'I haven't finished my Tyrannosaurus Rex.' His voice echoed loudly through the reading room. The knitting woman frowned like it was a normal day at the library. I didn't care. I grabbed Max and pulled him off the chair. A rainbow of pencils rolled across the table. I looked back at the noise of them falling onto the floor. Then I saw inside the back of the van. There were only boxes and trolleys and normal-looking people. The other people in the library started talking again. I guess they'd thought the same as me.

'Sorry, Max!' I whispered and I gathered up his pencils. 'See, they're not broken.'

'Why did you do that?'

'What?'

'Why did you grab me?'

'Sorry, Max,' I said again and he climbed back onto his chair. I never had anyone little to take care of before, but I thought it would be a good idea not to say anything about the soldiers with machine guns I had imagined sitting in the back of the van.

The people from the van wheeled the boxes inside on trolleys and started taking books off the shelves. Not just a few books for reading at home after dinner; they were taking a lot of books, and even though they weren't soldiers, I felt like something bad was happening. The State Library was not a lending library. You were only supposed to look at the books while you were there.

I remembered what Billy said about getting an education. The only thing I wanted to learn about was art, that's what I was good at. I couldn't go back to school now, so I figured I'd have to learn from books. I went to the art section and got three big books, one about Monet and one about Vincent van Gogh, and then I saw one about Leonardo da Vinci so I took that too. I hid them in a cleaner's cupboard next to the men's toilets, and got one of our blankets to cover them. When I'd finished I sat down beside Max and I heard one of the people from the van telling the eyebrow woman that she was from Friends of the Library. She had a box full of books on her trolley.

'We'll take as many as we can and keep them safe until it's all over,' I heard her say. My heart was beating fast and I felt sick. I'd pinched plenty of other things, but never anything so valuable. These books were gold. They had dust jackets and shiny pages and plenty of coloured pictures. I told myself I needed them, like the food I'd pinched and the coins I'd used to make my getaway and the chalks for my education. But deep down I knew I'd stolen them because I wanted them. I'd become a thief.

Max turned a page. 'They're Grandpa's cows,' he said like he hadn't even noticed I'd been gone.

I looked down and saw a picture of some white cows with black spots. They were standing in long green grass and the sky was pure blue.

'How many has he got?' I said, trying not to think about the books.

'A lot . . . more than ten, I think.'

'Where does he keep them?' I hadn't asked anyone this many questions for a long time. Once I started I couldn't stop.

'Gulliver's Meadows.'

'That's not a place!'

'Yes it is. It's Grandpa's place. It's his farm.'

'But what's the town called?'

'There isn't a town, just paddocks.'

'There's gotta be a town. Where's it near?'

Max wrinkled his forehead. 'It's past a mountain.' He waved his hand. 'You know, near the great big railway tunnel. When is Billy coming back?'

'Soon,' I said and I hoped my answer would come true. I stopped asking Max questions and tried to remember what it was like to be six and to know only the most important things; like having a grandpa who lived near a great big railway tunnel and owned more than ten cows.

I watched the Friends of the Library loading boxes of books into the van. Then some people came out of the foyer carrying a person between them, one at the head and one at the feet. You couldn't tell if the person was alive or not. They were loading it into the van when Max turned around to see what I was looking at.

'Is that person dead?' he asked me.

'I don't know.'

They closed the doors of the van and drove off. Not long after, Billy came.

'Did you get banana fritters?' Max asked.

'No fritters today, but I got some other good things.' Billy talked quietly and he didn't let us look in his bag straight away. 'Let's go outside and have our lunch,' he said. 'I think the sun's almost shining.'

Billy had already picked the place. He pointed to a seat that was sheltered from the wind. It was the only spot along the wall where no one could see you from inside the library or from the street. I thought Max would notice, but he didn't say anything. Maybe he was too hungry.

Billy undid his bag. He had cans with ring-pull lids. The labels were burnt off them, so it was like a lucky dip. Billy got baked beans and Max and me got fruit salad. We didn't have spoons so Billy ate his beans off his pocketknife. It took him a long time because the beans kept falling off and he had to be extra careful not to cut his tongue. Max and me drank the juice and then picked the pieces of fruit out of the cans with our fingers. I got two cherries.

'Do you like cherries?' I asked Max.

'I don't know.'

I gave him one to taste, and he nibbled it and nodded so I gave him the other one. Next there was bread and dried sausage. Something hot would have been better, something like Sam's Kebabs, but I knew Billy would have done his best. I ate the bread and put the sausage in my pocket.

'Eat up, Skip,' Billy said.

I told him about the eyebrow woman, who'd been kind to us. 'I thought she might like a bit of sausage,' I said.

'Eat it. I can't feed everyone.'

As well as the food, Billy got a beanie for Max. It was dark blue with white stripes and a picture of a cat. The Cats were Max's favourite football team. Last of all Billy gave me a new packet of chalk.

'Don't let anything stop you, Skip,' he said.

I nearly told him about the books then, but I didn't want Max to know I was a thief.

Not as many people stayed that night. I heard someone say it was safer outside. But Billy and Max and me got in our bunker. The planes sounded close and Billy didn't put his torch on. Max sang 'Incy Wincy Spider' for a little while. I could feel him doing the actions in the dark. Then he went to sleep. I thought about the cows in Max's Book of After-school Activities, and about his grandpa who lived on the other side of the mountain at Gulliver's Meadows, just near the big railway tunnel. I visualised meeting a cow in person, with green grass right up to its kneecaps. That made me think about other things I wanted to see, like stars reflected in rivers and irises growing by sunlit ponds. I was just thinking about how good it would be to have a dog that I could paint on a plate, when Max started screaming.

He thrashed around under the blanket like he was having a fit. Billy pushed one of the tables over and we dragged him out of the bunker. We talked to him, trying to calm him down. But he wouldn't shut up and his legs and arms kicked like crazy. People were calling out in the dark, 'What's the matter? What's going on?'

I threw myself down on top of Max, pinning his arms to his sides and Billy knelt beside him, stroking his hair, talking quietly. Someone else came and sat next to us. I couldn't see who it was till Billy put his torch on. It was the eyebrow woman. She felt Max's forehead and pulled back his eyelids.

'He's dreaming, poor lamb,' she said. 'Night Terrors, that's what it is. He'll be fine in a minute.'

At last I felt Max stop fighting, and I moved off him. He opened his eyes and tears rolled down his cheeks.

'When will Mummy come, Skip?'

I didn't know if God would listen to the prayers of a thief, and I didn't know if you could undo prayers once you'd said them, but I tried. I even offered to do a deal with God. I said if Max's mum came through the door I'd put the books back on the shelves. I didn't want Max to be like me, always looking and never finding.

7

Albert Park

Most people believe their mother will come for them when she says she will. They don't think of all the reasons why she mightn't be able to, especially the reason of war. It isn't a thing you think will happen to you, especially when you're six years old. It's an *unlikely event*. Max thought about his mother the way other people think about the sun; because it was there yesterday, it would shine again tomorrow.

'She's gone shopping,' he told us on the first day. 'She goes shopping at night after work. I stay here at the library until she comes back, and I don't go outside. Sometimes she buys me fish fingers for my dinner.'

On the second day he said, 'She might come tomorrow.' And when she didn't come again, he said, 'She might come next Tuesday.'

After a few days, Max and me thought of a plan to find his mum. Max had a photo of her stuck in his book. In the mornings, before people went away to find food, Max and me showed everyone the photo. Max carried the book and I did the talking. 'This is Max's mum,' I'd say. 'If you see her anywhere, would you please tell her that Max is still waiting in the library?'

Cecily, the eyebrow lady, thought it was a great idea. We showed the photo every day in case the old people forgot what Mrs Montgomery looked like, and for the new arrivals.

Most days someone new came. Some of them brought pots and pans and blankets and tiny gas burners like the ones people take camping. They arranged chairs and desks like cubbyhouses. It was always cold. Wind gusted through the holes in the walls and people hacked pieces off the carpet and burnt them to keep warm.

Max was brave. He only cried at night, and he cried quietly. I wouldn't have known he did it, except one night I felt his hands wiping the tears off his cheeks. Sometimes I had to think about my overcoat list or do my visualisation technique because it's a difficult circumstance when you've got a small boy crying quietly beside you and you don't know what to do. I hated the quiet crying even more than the screaming nightmares that he had almost every night.

I shifted the art books to higher ground when the toilets started flushing backwards. After about a week, the water stopped altogether and the smell got so bad that people started moving out. Some said the smell was coming from the toilets. Others said it was the bodies of the people who'd been killed when the front of the library collapsed. People argued about everything. The Friends of the Library stopped coming, although there were still thousands of books on the shelves.

'We've got to find somewhere else soon, Skip,' Billy said.

He didn't have to tell me that. Every morning another building had disappeared from the horizon. They weren't all bombed; some just crumpled quietly, like a pair of jeans with no legs in them, because there was nothing to hold them up.

I looked at Max, who was drawing in his book. 'What are we going to tell Max?'

Billy shrugged his shoulders. 'The truth, he'll have to get used to it.'

After that, I never left Max and Billy by themselves for a second. I had to be there when Billy told Max we were leaving. I wanted to hear the words so I'd know if it was just Billy and me going or all three of us. Max didn't argue when Billy said we'd have to find another place to stay, and he didn't cry when Billy told him his mother might not come. He just kept on drawing and said, 'Mummy always came for me before.'

Billy said we needed another tactic. That's when I knew we were taking Max along. 'We've got to get his mind off his mother.'

'Why don't we think of some places we could go?' I said. 'Things Max would like to see.'

'Like what?'

'Trains? He loves trains. He's got heaps of pictures in his book. We could take him to the station for a visit, to get him used to being away from here.'

Most of the people who were there when we first came to the library had gone. Every day more people left. Sometimes others came, but not many. I finally got the nerve to tell Billy what I'd done, but I let him think I only did it to keep the books safe, like the Friends of the Library. He didn't say if what I'd done was right or wrong, but he found me a suitcase with wheels to put the books in.

On the day we planned to take Max to look at the trains I got the books out of their hiding-place and put them in my case. Then I went to say goodbye to Cecily. Even though Billy never said so, I had a feeling we wouldn't be coming back.

'Come with us, Cecily. We're like sitting ducks up here,' I said, repeating the words I'd overheard that morning.

She laughed softly and shook her head. 'Don't worry about me, Skip, where I'm going, nothing can hurt me.'

I gave her the end of the dried sausage that I'd been saving for emergencies. Her lips curved and her eyes sparkled under her soaring eyebrows and she put her bony arms around me. They felt like wings, and I remembered someone telling me once that you turn into an angel when you die. I wondered if Cecily knew the rules for praying. I wanted to ask her if you could reverse a prayer or if you had to be a good person before God would take any notice. But I couldn't because there was a lump in my throat, and in my head was a picture of Cecily flying away. I closed my eyes and she whispered something into my hair.

'Remember, Skip,' she said, 'that home is where your winter coat is.'

I didn't understand right away what she meant. But her words soaked through my skull like warm oil, behind my eyes, down my spine and into the empty space inside me.

There was one last thing I wanted to do before we left. I went outside and drew a picture of Michaela on a patch

of broken footpath. It was the first time I'd drawn anything since the flowers and cross I did for Bradley Clark
when I thought he was Billy. I'd never done a portrait. For
Michaela's face I drew a pond. I drew irises for her eyes,
and for her lips I did a small pink rosebud lying on its side.
Then I went inside and told Billy I was ready.

But Max wasn't. He wanted to see the trains but he
was afraid his mother might come while he was gone. He
screamed and kicked and cried and bit Billy on the hand.
I promised him a ride on my suitcase with wheels, but he
wouldn't shut up. Billy and me didn't know what to do.
Then Cecily and the knitting lady came to see what was
going on.

'I'll watch out for your mum,' Cecily told Max. She
closed her eyes and stroked his head and said the words
over and over like a magic spell. Max's muscles relaxed
and his face faded from red to pink, like the sun was going
down under his skin, and at last he stopped crying. He lay
still and the knitting lady, who didn't like noise and never
even talked to us before, leant over and gave him something. It was a pair of striped mittens with button eyes and
stitched-on smiles.

There was a 7-Eleven store on the corner, across the
road from the station. We went shopping there before

we caught the train, except we didn't have to pay. There wasn't much to choose from because the store had been looted, like any others that weren't flattened or burnt out. You could tell which people were already scared of running out of food. They were the ones who took as much as they could carry, instead of only what they needed. Most of the things we got were in cans with the labels burnt off. We knew sardines because they were in flat tins, and we got muesli bars that were only a bit melted because they were in foil packs.

We put our shopping in Billy's backpack, crossed the road and walked downstairs to Platform One. It was dark and cold underground, but there were fires burning and people cooking on them. It was ages since we'd had anything hot to eat, and whatever was cooking smelt delicious. I didn't know I'd started walking slow until Billy called out. 'It's rats,' he said, then he laughed.

The subway people had lived underground for a long time, not just since the war came. They lived in tunnels where the trains didn't go any more. There were old people and young ones and even little children. Some were musicians and others were dancers, jugglers or fire-eaters. I saw the guy with the barbed-wire tattoo, who drew pictures in the mall, and Billy spoke to some of the others as we walked by.

We decided not to go in a VFT, which stands for Very Fast Train, because we wanted to enjoy the scenery, and everything goes past in a blur when you're on a VFT. There were people already in some of the carriages. We walked to the locomotive, where the engine-driver sits, and Billy slid his pocketknife in a crack and made the door come open. We let Max drive. I looked out the windows and saw white cows with black spots. When we got to the tunnel, Billy lifted Max up so he could pull the lever that sounded the whistle. We got out at the station near Gulliver's Meadows. Billy opened all the tins and we found we had yellow peaches set in jelly, dog food, beetroot and some sweet, sticky stuff called condensed milk. I thought about Pablo Picasso's dog, when we opened the dog food, and wished I could have saved it until I got a dog of my own. We sat in a paddock full of green grass and ate the peaches and the beautiful silver sardines, and dipped our fingers in the condensed milk and licked them, and then I drew some cows on the platform for Max and a sausage dog for me, before we caught the train home again.

I never had anyone to pretend with before. My dad never pretended. Even though I only did it for Max, our make-believe train ride had been fun. It stopped me wondering about things like weapons of max destruction and where we were going to sleep and why Max's mother hadn't come and what would happen to us all next.

We followed Billy down to the guard's van. 'We'll sleep in here tonight,' he said.

Max looked up at him. 'Aren't we going to the library?'

'It's too dark to go back now,' Billy said.

Max looked at me and I felt bad. I'd told him we were only coming for a visit, but deep down I'd guessed that this was what Billy would do. I got myself ready for Max to throw another tantrum, but he looked at his mittens for a while and nothing happened. I guessed he was thinking about what Cecily said. I took the books out of my suitcase and Billy and me made a bed in it for Max, and zipped the cover up halfway so he could breathe and keep warm at the same time. I lay down on the bench beside him and Billy sat in a corner with his back against the wall. I closed my eyes and thought about the four storeys of books that we'd left behind, and wondered how many pages that would be and how many paragraphs and sentences and words and letters.

It was quiet in the guard's van except for the faraway stutter of machine-gun fire, but after a while something made me think Max was crying. I reached out in the dark and took the handle of my suitcase on wheels and I rocked it backwards and forwards beside me, the way I'd seen mothers do with babies in prams. Then I heard

Billy's harmonica sounding sweet and sad and blue all at the same time, like a train whistle in the night. The music soaked into my skin and bones and I felt myself falling down and down and down into the velvet dark.

That night I dreamt of Cecily. She was flying around a church steeple. I couldn't see her face, but I knew it was her because of the coffee tin under one wing. She was chucking biscuits everywhere and soldiers were firing machine guns at her. I screamed, trying to make her fly away, but she said, 'I promised Max I'd look out for his mother.' When the bullets hit her, she didn't fall down, she exploded into billions of stars.

Then Billy was there, shaking me, and I knew something had happened.

'Wake up, Skip. It's morning.'

I knew it was more than that. Everything was vibrating, the carriage doors rattled and there was a rumbling sound like a huge train was going to smash through the subway wall. We woke Max and shoved the books and blankets in my case, then we all hurried up the stairs to see what was going on. Most people were going the other way, rushing towards the underground. The platform at ground level was almost deserted, except for the subway people, and even they looked like they were getting ready to move on to someplace else.

'Keep off the streets,' the fire-eater said when he saw us. 'The place is swarmin' with tanks.'

'I was there, man, I seen it all,' someone else said, 'and I swear to God it wasn't random bombing, it was pinpoint precision.'

'What was the target?' asked Billy.

'State Library, man. There ain't one brick left standin' on another.'

Precision is the opposite of random, and random is the same as hit-and-miss. I couldn't think of a reason why anyone would want to bomb the State Library. Was this my fault? Was this how God had answered my prayer? I held Max's hand tight and squeezed my eyelids shut.

'If youse are leavin' town, the safest way is to follow the railway tracks,' the fire-eater told Billy. 'There's road-blocks everywhere and it'll only get worse.'

We sat on a red couch in the travellers' lounge and opened up Max's book like a travel brochure. Max turned the pages. He pointed to a photograph. 'That's Disney-land. We could go there,' he said.

'It's a bit far away,' said Billy.

'What about here, then,' said Max flipping through the pages. 'Is this too far?'

'Dreamland,' said Billy looking at the postcard in Max's book. 'Great choice, Max. It's near the beach.'

Dreamland was a fun park. The entrance looked like a man's head, with a wide-open mouth full of big, white teeth. There were palm trees and blue skies in the picture and a Ferris wheel. It looked like somewhere you might go for a holiday.

Billy looked up at the clock on the wall as though we were going to catch a train. It was eight-thirty. 'I've walked there before,' he said. 'We could probably make it in a few hours.'

The first part of our journey was underground. There were stacks of other people walking in the same direction as us. It wasn't light enough to see them properly. I imagined we were an army; an army of old people, of mothers and fathers, of children and babies and of people who didn't belong. The Army of the Third Side, unarmed because we didn't believe in war.

I wondered if all the others were going to Dreamland, and I listened, but they only talked about what had already happened. At the end of the underground the metal tracks stretched out in front of us, dead electricity wires striped the pigeon-grey sky and rain dribbled down on us.

'Is this the way to Dreamland?' Max asked Billy.

'Yes.'

'Have you been there before?'

'Yes, I told you.'

'How many times?'

'Lots of times.'

'How far is it?'

'A long way.'

In the beginning we went fast because we wanted to get to Dreamland. The rain made the metal tracks slippery, so we walked on the stones beside them. When Max got tired I let him sit on top of my case, but bits of rock kept jamming the wheels, and even though Billy was slow I kept getting further and further behind. All the other people on the track had passed us a long time back. I guess we'd been walking for at least a couple of hours when the rain started pelting down. Billy turned around and shouted to us. I couldn't hear what he said, but he was pointing up ahead. He waited till Max and me caught up.

'There's a tunnel a bit further along,' he said. 'We'll take a break when we get there.'

Orange flames flickered in the gloom. 'A fire,' I said. 'Maybe someone's already in there.'

Billy made us wait and went ahead. After a few seconds he waved to Max and me, and we knew it was safe.

'Got any smokes?' asked the man in the tunnel when we were all inside. Billy only had one cigarette left, so they took it in turns. We crouched around the old man's fire while the rain poured down outside. Steam came off our coats and out of our mouths, and I thought about peace pipes and American Indians and Chief Seattle.

'Most folks don't stop,' the man said when they got down to the brown part of the cigarette. 'They're all in a hurry to get where they're goin'. I hear they're headin' north. They reckon there's a place for people wiv nowhere else to go. You headed that way?'

'Maybe.'

'Where you from?'

'City, Queen's Elbows.'

'Yeah? Queen's Elbows. Been there meself a few times. Nice place.'

'Not any more,' said Billy. 'They flattened it.'

'Yeah? So where you stayin' now?'

'Here and there,' said Billy.

'Like me eh? Don't like to stay in one place too long, 'specially not now. Must be tough with the little bloke, though.'

He leant his head towards Max and Max did something I didn't expect. He said, 'I'm Max and I'm six and this is Billy and Skip.'

I looked at Billy, but it was too late. Max had made a mistake but it wasn't his fault; he didn't know we never told strangers our names, even my running-away name.

'Billy, Skip and Max, pleased to meet youse all,' the man said. 'And I'm Albert, Albert Park.' Then he laughed and he looked like the picture of Dreamland on Max's postcard, except he didn't have as many teeth and they were yellowish-brown, not white. As he laughed I realised Albert Park wasn't his name at all, it was the name of a suburb. He must have thought our names were made-up too, so it didn't matter about Max's mistake.

'Fancy a cuppa?' Albert pulled a dirty rag out of his pocket and wrapped it around his hand, then he reached over the fire and picked up a can of boiling water like he was invincible or something. We shared the rest of yesterday's muesli bars with Albert and he shared his one tea bag with us. He only had two tin mugs, so we took it in turns and in between he squeezed the tea bag and put it in his pocket.

'What's in the case, lad?' Albert asked me.

'Books,' I said. 'About famous painters.'

'Skip's an artist,' said Billy. 'He draws beautiful pictures. Why don't you draw something on Mr Park's tunnel for him, Skip?'

Billy and Albert talked quietly while I stared at the

sooty walls through the dancing flames. I heard Billy say something about Dreamland and Albert talked about some other place called No-Man's-Land. Then I heard nothing as I began to draw the wild creatures I saw in my head. I drew buffalo and elk and caribou and wolves, and then I drew God's red children, which is what Chief Seattle called his people even though they were really a brownish colour. I gave them horses to ride and head-dresses made of eagles' feathers to wear. I gave their horses a prairie, and I put gallop in their legs, wind in their manes and breath in their nostrils. I gave their riders bows and arrows to hunt with. They were precision weapons, because God's red children only took what they needed. Then I drew red hearts inside all the bodies: in the men and in the animals. The last thing I did was put my hand against the wall and draw around it. That's like a signature. When I took my eyes away from my drawing I felt surprised I was in a railway tunnel. I don't know if Albert liked my picture, because it was *primitive*. That's what ancient drawings are sometimes called, especially when they're found on the walls of caves. A railway tunnel isn't much different from a cave, except it's open at both ends and most caves are not.

I could tell that Max liked my picture. 'Can I draw around my hand?' he asked and I gave him a piece of chalk. He traced the outline of his hand and wrote his name underneath in big crooked letters. Then he put black stripes across his cheeks with the soot from his fingers, and I promised to look for an eagle's feather for him.

After the rain stopped a few people walked by and Billy asked Albert what the time was. Albert peered at his watch. 'Gettin' on for eleven-thirty,' he said.

'We'd better get a move on, then.'

'Remember; you take the left spur to dodge No-Man's-Land.'

I didn't hear what Billy said because Max ran outside and started making Indian war cries and I had to run after him. The people on the tracks ahead of us turned around.

'You've gotta be quiet, Max,' I said, 'the enemy might be hiding just over the horizon.'

I said it like it was a game, so Max would play along. I didn't want him to know how scared I was that my words would come true.

8

The Carousel of War and Peace

We came to a fork where the rails curved away in different directions. There were no signposts, only numbers. The people in front of us all went left, but Billy led us the other way, through a deep concrete cutting smothered with graffiti. We walked between the walls, like ants between the pages of a comic. If there'd been no war and we weren't trying to find someplace safe to stay, I would have stopped and looked at the graffiti, the way people stare at art in galleries.

The longer we walked the more distant the sounds of fighting became. I couldn't hear much at all; no voices, no cars, nothing except stones clattering down the steep embankments beside the tracks, and my suitcase wheels bumping over the sleepers. I thought we'd never get to

Dreamland. I couldn't stop thinking Billy might have made a mistake. Maybe we should have gone the way the other people had. Would it be better to turn around and go back? I didn't dare say anything to Billy. Every time Max asked him a question, he got grumpier and quieter.

Sometimes we'd pass a ladder bolted to the wall. I wanted to climb up and have a look. I hated the silence. I wanted to shout, 'Who's there?' I wanted to fill our ears with sound.

'Let's sing something,' I said to Max.

'What do you want to sing?'

'Anything.'

But Billy shushed us with a finger to his lips.

Max and me were tired of walking and not getting anywhere, and I couldn't even be bothered looking at the graffiti on the walls. I wished we were back in the library with Cecily and that last night had never happened. When you concentrate on wishing for things you can't have, you miss out on clues that something good might be just around the corner. I didn't notice the concrete walls sloping away and I didn't see the gulls swirling like scraps of paper in the sky, so I was gobsmacked when we walked out of the cutting and saw Dreamland.

It looked even better than on Max's postcard. Behind the fun park, a boardwalk edged the yellow sand beside a shallow, sheltered bay.

'Wait here,' Billy said, so Max and me sat on my case on the little platform, staring at Dreamland. It was one-thirty when I looked at the clock on the other side of the train tracks. It took Billy five minutes to reach the entrance to the fun park. He limped down a steep triangle of grass between the road and the station, crossed the main street and walked along the footpath toward the yawning mouth. We watched him disappear inside and waited, hardly daring to blink in case we missed him. Another five minutes went by and then it was ten and at last Billy was there, waving to us.

I grabbed Max's hand and the handle of my case. We ran like crazy down the green hill, looked both ways although there wasn't a car in sight, darted across the wide black stretch of tar and sprinted along the footpath. When we walked under the big teeth we laughed out loud, we just couldn't help it. This time Billy didn't tell us to stop.

There were plenty of feathers at Dreamland. They were carved on a golden eagle on the carousel. The eagle was on the front of a chariot, with its giant wings spread out. It was bigger than Max.

'It's a Roman war chariot,' said Billy, 'and there's one on the other side that's called the peace chariot.'

Max and me ran around to see. Instead of an eagle on the front, it had a lady with a peaceful look carved on her wooden face. As well as the two chariots, the carousel had sixty-eight horses.

'The theme of the carousel is war and peace,' Billy said. 'Look at the cherubs.' He pointed to a carving of a fat baby angel. 'Thirty-six cherubs,' he said, and then he showed us the painted flowers and butterflies. I never heard Billy talk so much before. He knew everything about the Carousel of War and Peace. 'It's very old,' he said. 'Been here since the year nineteen hundred and twenty-three.'

Max had already got on one of the horses, but I didn't. I was waiting to see if Billy would tell us more. I'd got used to not asking questions, and waiting for signs that Billy had something he wanted to say. He was stroking his beard. That was usually a sign. I was right. 'Wars come and wars go,' he said. 'Things change, but the carousel is always here. It reminds people of the good times.'

'Come on, Skip! Get on!' Max yelled.

Billy smiled as Max pulled himself up on the platform, so I got on too. I picked a light grey horse with black blotches.

'That's called a pinto,' Billy said. It had a red harness and silver horseshoes.

Max was on a black horse in front of the chariot of war. 'Let's be Indians!' he said and he grabbed the reins and clicked his tongue against his teeth. 'Giddy up, Midnight!' he yelled.

That's when Billy started acting strange. He put his hands up to his mouth like a loudspeaker and started calling out into the empty fun park like it was crammed full of people. 'Step right up, boys and girls, and ride the merry-go-round. Two nights only. Don't miss out. Tell all your friends. Come on now, don't be shy. The merry's perfectly safe, mothers and fathers, let your little ones enjoy the ride of a lifetime. Step right up. Get your tickets here! You won't get better value anywhere. Step this way!' It was like Billy had been doing this job all his life.

After he'd finished telling Max and me to hang on tight, Billy sat down in the chariot of peace and took his harmonica out of his pocket. It was small and silver and its name was Hohner. I'd seen that written on the top, among all the looping, swirling patterns. Once, Billy played his Hohner outside St Mary's. It was Anzac Day. He sat down on the steps and shut his eyes and played. Billy didn't play for money. If he'd wanted money he would have gone to the mall, where buskers go. I don't know why he played his music at St Mary's that day but I wondered if he was like me, and never knew what to say to God, so he played his music instead. Some of the people who went to church that day didn't go inside.

They stayed and listened to Billy instead. It was like a magic spell was on them and they couldn't leave. Sometimes, when I look at Monet's paintings, it's like a spell is on me and I can't walk away.

Billy curled his hands around his Hohner. I got ready for the magic. He closed his eyes and started to play. My feet slid into the stirrups, I took the reins in my hands and a shout burst out of me like fireworks. 'Come away, Captain Moonlight, come away!' My shout went up and over the Ferris wheel and down the other side. I felt the horse's powerful muscles move and I thought of the leopard on Archimedes's chest.

Max and me didn't see the grey clouds rolling in because we were having the ride of our lives, galloping over the grassy plains, chasing buffalo and elk and caribou and listening to the wolves howling in the mountains. But Billy did. After a while he wrapped his Hohner in a piece of rag and put it in his pocket. Then everything went back to the way it was. We got off the carousel to look at the other things in Dreamland before the rain came.

We passed the House of Horrors and Sideshow Alley, where the tin ducks were, and then we looked at the Ferris wheel and the dodgem cars, but I didn't feel like pretending any more; I wanted to do something real.

Then Max said, 'Have you got something we can eat, Billy?'

Billy looked in his backpack but all we had left was a tin of sardines and some jelly snakes. 'There are shops up there on the Boulevard,' he said, pointing. Three flights of concrete steps with metal handrails ran from behind the station to the top of the hill, where we could see a row of houses and shops and more palm trees. 'We'd better see what we can find before it gets dark.'

I read the signs outside Dreamland. 'Steep Gradient. 15 mins to Shopping Centre', said the one pointing towards the steps. I knew Billy would have trouble. 'You wait here, Billy, I'll go,' I said.

It didn't take him long to get back to being grumpy. 'Since when did you start telling me what to do?'

'I just thought, all those stairs . . . and there's no one around. I'd be okay.'

'You mean you haven't seen anyone,' he said.

We ended up all walking beside the road that cork-screwed up the steep slope from Dreamland to the Boulevard. By the time we got there the rain clouds had moved on. I looked at the peacock sea and the violet sky. The tunnel where we'd sheltered from the rain with Albert Park was flyspeck-small and the rails were snail-silver. Further away still were the hazy outlines of the city, and warships in the docks. It had taken us roughly four hours to get to Dreamland, but I couldn't help thinking it wouldn't take very long in a tank or a plane, or even if you were a soldier who didn't have arthritis in his leg, or a small boy on a suitcase to pull.

'I'm hungry,' Max reminded us as we walked under the palm trees to where the road was blocked with lumps of concrete and barriers of red-and-white mesh. I didn't like this place. It was too quiet. But the others went under the barrier and I had to follow them past the houses with neat white fences, striped blinds and shiny doorknockers, and past a big hotel where you couldn't see in the windows because of the reflections of sea and sky and us. I wanted to ask Billy where everyone had gone. Where were the people who owned the nice houses? Were they watching us, wondering which side we were on or if we had come to steal from them, or worse?

Max walked in front of me with his hand in Billy's. I didn't want to be last, but the wheels of my suitcase made a noise if I walked fast. I almost wished for the sounds of war machines and bullets and bombs and shouting and matching black boots on the footpath. At least I could have breathed properly without worrying that someone would hear me. Instead, I walked slowly and breathed quietly and said nothing.

There was no 7-Eleven store on the Boulevard, but further back we found a narrow street full of cafes and other shops. And there were people, soft-talking, soft-walking people, fluttering down the darkening street, in and out of doorways like velvet-winged moths. Some waited outside the shops while others went inside, or darted into the bakery or the shop with rows and rows of cakes in the window. We went into the fruit shop first. Most things were rotten, but we got apples and carrots, a few bananas and some bottled water. In the newsagency Billy found a whole box of batteries, a cigarette lighter and a packet of lollies, but all the cigarettes were gone. We packed everything in my suitcase, on top of the art books.

Then Billy said, 'We'll have to get a move on. I'll go to the cake shop and you boys see if you can find some paper for drawing on.'

It was dark inside the butcher's shop and I made Max wait outside while I ran back to get a loan of Billy's torch. One of the shadow people was talking to him. He stopped when he saw me coming, but not before I heard him say something about a place Albert Park had mentioned, 'No-Man's-Land'. I made up my mind to ask Billy about it when he was in a good mood.

'You'd better come in with me,' I said to Max, 'I'll need someone to hold the torch.' There was plenty of paper on the counter in the butcher's shop. I rolled it up and was putting it in a plastic bag when Max wandered off. I heard him calling from the back of the shop. He shone the torch so I could see where he was. 'Let's see what's in there.' He was standing in front of a white door.

'It's probably just a kitchen,' I said. 'Come on, Billy will be waiting.'

'Just a peek,' said Max with his hand on the latch. 'It won't take long.'

I should have stopped Max right then, but I watched his fingers undo the metal catch. The door was heavy and Max couldn't open it by himself. I wish I'd walked away, but I didn't. I stuck my fingers underneath the rubber seal and pulled. The door came open with a rush and Max screamed. I grabbed the torch and turned it off, but not before we'd seen all the dead bodies hanging from a rail on huge metal hooks, and not before we'd seen what the maggots had done to them. The smell was disgusting. I tried not to breathe, and Max was throwing up all over the place. I grabbed his hand and we ran for the street.

'They're animals, Max,' I said in case he thought they were people's bodies.

'I know,' he sobbed, 'the poor things.'

Billy came back with bread and cake and biscuits and he held out a jam tart each for Max and me. 'Thought you were starving,' he said when we didn't take them. I told him what we'd seen and he got a bottle of water out and cleaned Max up as good as he could. I got a bottle for myself, but no matter how hard I scrubbed or how much water I used I felt like the smell of the rotten animals had got into my skin and onto my clothes.

We walked back the way we came, and even though it was dark there were no lights burning inside the houses. They were like people without hearts; raspberry tarts without the jam. The further we got away from the butcher's shop, the better I felt. I saw Dreamland, milky as the moon, maybe only fifteen minutes away if we walked fast. Carelessly, I let my suitcase wheels hum along the pavement in time with my heart.

We had got to the S-bend in front of the hotel when suddenly Billy put his arms out and grabbed me and Max and we all went tumbling down the grassy embankment. I saw streamers of starlight, smelt dirt up close and felt my back smack against something hard. I caught my breath and rolled over, looking for the others and for my case. A low stone wall had stopped us from rolling onto the winding road, two metres below. Max was lying face-down on the grass above me. He was sobbing. I don't think I could hear him, but I knew, somehow. I crawled up and lay next to him.

'What's the matter?' I whispered.

'I've lost my glasses.'

'We'll find them. I'll get Billy's torch.'

Then I heard a motor running, the gears changing at the bottom of the hill.

'Keep your head down!' Billy hissed. I saw the lights of a truck and ducked.

We lay flat beside the wall, while the truck wound its way slowly towards the top of the hill. Once it passed us, Billy put his head up and so did Max and me. We watched the hotel gates slide open to let the truck go through and saw lights flood the building. We waited for a long time before we dared use the torch to look for Max's glasses and my case.

That night we slept in the House of Horrors. We'd checked it out while it was light. From outside it looked like a huge, lumpy cave. Inside was a miniature railway. It had everything: tracks, a platform, signals, tunnels and a tiny train. We walked along the tracks with Billy's torch and looked at the fake skeletons, bats, witches, ghosts, giant spiders and monsters. Bits of cloth, hanging from the ceiling, brushed against our faces, and if you shut your eyes they felt exactly like spider webs. It must have been fantastic when everything worked. Billy said there were ghostly noises, special lighting effects and coloured smoke. We planned to sleep in the carriages. They all had names painted on them. Max and me had picked the Devil's Lair and Billy said he'd have the Vampire's Nest.

Before we got in our carriages that night, Billy hung his torch up and fixed Max's glasses with a bandaid. He always had useful things in his pockets, like his pocket-knife and bandaids and bits of string and dead Christmas beetles, which aren't exactly useful but they're nice to look at. After Billy fixed the glasses, Max and me got our appetites back. The bananas were a bit squashed, so we ate them first, then we had rainbow cake with chocolate icing and hundreds and thousands.

Billy didn't want any cake. 'Save me some for breakfast,' he said. 'And don't forget to switch the torch off before you go to sleep.'

I thought of asking Billy about No-Man's-Land, but decided to wait until Max wasn't around. I hung Dad's coat up on a nail in the wall and Max and me got in our carriage and shared a blanket. The ghosts didn't worry us; we knew they were only make-believe.

Max didn't say anything for a while and I got nervous. I thought he might ask me a question I didn't know the answer to. I started talking so he couldn't. 'Tomorrow we'll fix this place up a bit, Max,' I said. 'We'll patch up the holes in the walls and sweep the platform. We'll make it real nice.'

Then I opened the packet of Clinkers from the newsagent's and we played a game. We each put a Clinker in our mouth and then we sucked the chocolate off and tried to guess what colour the inside was. I like pink ones best but there aren't many pink ones in a packet. In the game we had to say our answer out loud, then we both opened our mouths at the same time and I looked in Max's mouth and he looked in mine. The first one to get three guesses right was supposed to have a go of the cigarette lighter, even though Billy would have killed us if he knew. It's easy to tell the taste of green and pink, but sometimes yellow and orange are hard to tell apart. Max never got any right but I still let him have one go of the cigarette lighter. We could hear Billy snoring and we put our hands over our mouths so we wouldn't laugh.

After Max went to sleep I turned the torch off and had a go of the cigarette lighter. It looked like a candle burning in the dark. Candles always make me think about God, so I asked Him not to let Max dream about the poor dead animals. I hoped He'd forgotten about the other thing I asked.

I tried not to think about Cecily and the library, or about the lights in the hotel, the army truck and the

Boulevard of empty houses, or about the place called No-Man's-Land.

Instead, I thought about the way Billy was on the carousel that afternoon. I smiled in the dark when I thought of him shouting at the invisible crowd in a half-singing, half-talking sort of way. He was like a fishmonger at the market on a Saturday morning, trying to get rid of his King George whiting and his flathead and his gummy shark, so they didn't go off over the weekend.

I wished he'd be like that for ever, because it felt as though he enjoyed being with us. If he did, maybe he'd stay and I'd never be afraid of anything then. It would be perfect, just Billy and Max and me. I went to sleep then. I didn't know that the girl in the red coat would come and change everything.

9

One perfect day

In the salty grey morning I made a plan to give Billy and Max one perfect day. If it worked, maybe that would be enough to keep us together.

I needed to leave my books behind while I carried out the plan, and I wanted to make sure they'd be safe if anyone else should come to Dreamland while we were away. So, while Billy and Max slept, I crept deeper into the House of Horrors, carrying my suitcase. I followed the silver tracks into the Cavern of Vampires and then I turned Billy's torch on. I sat among the coffins and the dangling skeletons with Billy's torch in my hand and my books on my knees. I touched their shining covers and turned the cold, smooth pages and filled myself up with the look and the feel and the smell of the paper and pictures and words.

Then I opened the lid of one of the coffins and hid my books under Dracula's red-and-black cloak.

I promised myself that one day soon I'd read them again. I would get myself an education, like Billy said I must, but for now I had to concentrate on staying alive and keeping us together.

Billy and Max were still asleep when I got back, so I quietly collected the things I needed for one perfect day. Then I went outside and looked up towards the hotel. The night before it had shone like a lighthouse – we could still see it when we reached the House of Horrors – but in daylight it seemed a long way away. I couldn't see the metal gates or the truck, so I figured that if anyone was up there they wouldn't see me either. And anyway, where I was taking Billy and Max we'd be hidden by the walls of Dreamland.

I wheeled my case to the coffee-seller's booth behind the carousel. It had wheels and a canvas awning and shiny black doors under the counter. Billy had picked the lock with his pocketknife the day before, to see what was inside. We found small paper packets of salt, sugar, coffee, tea and powdered chocolate. There were spoons and cups and serviettes. I took what I needed and put them in my suitcase with the things I'd got from inside.

Then Billy woke up and came out and I asked him if we could spend the day at the beach. 'Please, Billy. I've got everything we need, look!' I showed him inside the suitcase.

It took him a long time to say anything.

'I know most people don't go to the beach in winter,' I said, 'but . . .'

'But we're not most people, are we, Skip?' he said. 'Now what you need is a good long-handled toasting fork.'

I ran inside to wake Max up, and Billy started making a toasting fork out of wire that was wrapped around one of the legs of the scenic railway. When everything was ready, we walked out underneath the big teeth and went down to the beach.

I tried to remember everything about that day. I heard the rush and sigh of small waves before I saw them and I felt glad because the sea is like the Carousel of War and Peace: it's always there.

Billy lit a fire on the sand beside the sea, and when my eyes crept up towards the Boulevard he said, 'They won't be able to see it from there, and anyway there's so many fires burning in this city, no one's gonna take any notice of a little one like ours.'

'Where are the ships, Billy?' asked Max.

'They can't come anywhere near here. The bay's too shallow.'

Billy's voice was smooth and yellow and peaceful, and it didn't matter at all that the sky was as grey as a pigeon's back. We spread our blankets on the damp sand and Billy boiled water in an empty peach can and made coffee and we sipped it from the stolen takeaway cups while we toasted our stale bread with the long-handled fork. Then we shared the last of our sardines and sprinkled them with salt from the paper packets.

After breakfast I found a feather for Max and stuck it in his football beanie, and even though it wasn't an eagle's feather he didn't mind. Then we borrowed Billy's peach can and built a sandcastle with twenty-seven turrets and a moat to keep the enemy out. Next we played cricket on the hard, wet sand until Billy hit a six with the driftwood bat and I saw my rolled-up football socks disappear into the sea. Max and me stripped our clothes off then and ran into the waves, and Billy laughed and shook his head and watched us go.

'Crazy kids! Crazy!'

'Crazeeeeeee!' we shouted back, and our voices sailed away like kite tails on the wind.

The crystal sea was freezing but we danced and ducked and dived. We were merchildren and we weren't afraid of the waves that crashed against our bodies and tried to drag us down. We saw Billy go searching up and down the long, straight beach like a pirate looking for buried treasure. We saw him discover driftwood sticks and drag them to the fire.

'Castaways!' I said to Max and punched the water with my fists. 'Castaways on a deserted island; you and me and Billy.'

'Castaways!' shouted Max.

Billy looked at us across the foaming waves and he got reckless and brave like Max and me; he piled the bleached wood on the leaping flames. Then he stood there on the shore with a blanket wrapped around him and his long grey whiskers flying like seaweed from his chin, and he roared at us like Neptune. We ran to him and we didn't care that we had no clothes on because we were wild creatures, Max and me. Then we lay down on a blanket as close to the fire as we dared. The flames flickered on our stormy-blue skins and made our hearts beat slow until we turned back into ordinary boys again. Then we put our clothes on and Billy baked bananas on the coals. When they were cooked we split them open and sprinkled them with cinnamon and chocolate powder and crystals of brown sugar that we'd got from the coffee-seller's stall, and we ate them out of their sizzling skins with plastic spoons.

Then the storm came and we stuffed everything into my case and hurried back to Dreamland. We lay in the ghost train, Max and me together in the Devil's Lair, warm and tired and sanded smooth. We whispered secrets to each other while rain battered the tin roof and thunder shook the world and Billy played his Hohner in the Vampire's Nest.

'I'm going to be a musician when I grow up,' Max said.

'What instrument are you going to play?'

'Violin. I've got a violin, only it's at my house.'

'Can you play it?'

'"Twinkle, Twinkle, Little Star."'

'Yeah?'

'I'm not very good yet. Mummy says you have to prac-tise every day to get good.'

I didn't want him to talk about his mother on that perfect day. 'What do you want to do tomorrow?'

'I think I'd like to go home.'

'We could go for another adventure.'

'We could go home first and then go for another adven-ture.'

'What if your mother wouldn't let you go?' I said and I felt Max grip my hand with one of his. 'It's your turn to choose tomorrow, Max. You can pick anywhere you like, anywhere.'

Max didn't answer straight away and I thought he was trying to decide. I didn't know he wanted to go home more than anything else in the whole universe, because that's something only people with homes can wish for. So I got a surprise when Max said in a small voice, 'I think I'd just like to go home, please.'

Billy stopped playing his harmonica then.

'Wait a few more days, Max,' he said, 'then we might be able to go back and see if they've put up the missing persons lists. Your mother might have put your name on the list. Then we can let her know where you are.'

The thought of Max finding his mother was as lonely as an albatross. I felt angry at how stupid I'd been. Max belonged to someone else and even Billy didn't belong to me. It didn't matter how perfect our day had been, it didn't change a thing.

When the rain let up a bit, I put Dad's coat on and went outside. I didn't tell the others where I was going. I walked across to the Ferris wheel and climbed up on the frame. It was easy, even though the white painted metal was wet and slippery. It was like running away; I just put one foot in front of the other one and didn't look back. When I got to the top I slid into the seat and pulled the padded armrest across in front of me.

You can see a long way from the top of the Ferris

wheel at Dreamland, but not as far as France or Gulliver's Meadows. All I could see was the wrecked city. Max and Billy came outside after a while. I wanted them to call out to me. I wished they would say, 'Skip, where are you Skip? Please . . . come home!' I watched them get on the carousel and I heard Billy calling out the way he did the day before: 'Step right this way folks, step right on up. Get your tickets here. Don't miss out now.'

Maybe he was remembering how he felt yesterday and maybe he wanted the feeling to never end. It was harder to get off the Ferris wheel, because I wasn't angry any more and because I had to look down. But Billy and Max waited for me.

'Just in the nick of time, young fella,' said Billy. 'I've got one ticket left to ride the pinto pony.' My feet slid into the stirrups and I took the reins in my hands the way I had the day before and the notes came out of Billy's harmonica and cast a spell over us all.

'Come away, Captain Moonlight, come away!' I whispered into my horse's wooden ear and my words went inside him and warmed his heart because that's what words do when people mean them; they get inside you and they change everything. I felt my horse's muscles moving and I felt breath go into him and out of him and I felt him swelling like the sea. When we stopped we were hungry so we headed back to the House of Horrors. That's when we saw the ballerina, walking through the misty rain towards the carousel.

We were gobsmacked to see her because not many people visit fun parks that don't work, especially when there's a war going on. Billy nodded at her but she climbed up on on a white horse without speaking, and I thought she mustn't know that a nod was like a 'hello' without words. Billy took us around behind the House of Horrors and we climbed in underneath the platform and I was glad we went that way because we had provisions and books in there and I didn't think it would be a good idea if other people knew where we were staying. We ate the rest of the rainbow cake and had a drink of water. Then we heard something cry out.

I looked out through the holes in the tin because I'd seen the lump under the girl's coat and I thought she might be having her baby right there on the carousel. She got down off her horse and her coat fell apart at the front because there were no buttons to put through the holes. She was already holding the baby and it had clothes on so I knew it must have been born some other time. The baby was crying, and the girl put one of her fingers in its mouth.

When she started to walk away I saw her coat had a hood, and I remembered a story I heard a long time ago, when I was just a little kid, about a girl with a coat like that. I knew it was only a made-up story, but when I saw the ballerina walk underneath the big teeth and out into the rain, I thought about the wolf in the story and I wondered where the girl was going and if she had a grand-mother to visit. It was getting late and cold, and I thought she looked too young to have a baby, but I didn't think we'd see them again.

10

The ballerina, the baby and the brave

Red is for danger.

Red was the colour of the ballerina's coat.

The next time we saw her she was sitting in the Chariot of Peace. We knew she was there because the baby was crying. Billy and Max and me heard it when we came back from looking for provisions.

For a day and a half after we'd been to the beach, the rain hardly stopped. Most of the time it bucketed down, and even if Max had made up his mind about his special outing we couldn't have gone. Most of the time we couldn't see any further than the roller-coaster but we could still hear muffled sounds. Whenever the rain let up we'd look out the skeleton's eyes to see what was happening up on the hill.

Weapons of Max destruction change scenery fast. They flattened the palm trees on the Boulevard so the roots scraped against the sky and the leafy tops were pressed flat into the ground like gigantic prehistoric fishbones. Loaded trucks crawled up the corkscrew road and soldiers stacked sandbags where the palm trees used to be. At night the lights came on in the hotel but during the day, even when it wasn't raining, you couldn't tell if anyone was watching from behind the shiny windows.

When the rain finally stopped we needed to find food. But first Billy bent a flap of tin on the back fence and made a secret entrance, so no one from the hotel could see our comings and goings, even if they had binoculars. We never went under the big teeth again. We walked along the boardwalk beside the sea, until we were out of sight of the hotel, before we crossed the road.

The supermarket was a lot further away than the shops behind the Boulevard. The front doors were boarded up, but the glass was smashed and it was easy to get underneath the planks. Inside it smelt disgusting because of the food rotting in the fridges and freezers. The shelves were almost empty, but there were a few people inside. I wondered where they came from. Were they like us, living somewhere they thought no one else would think of, or did they have homes to go to? They didn't look up when we came in, they just kept stuffing things in their bags like they were in the Great Supermarket Scramble or something.

We'd decided to hunt for canned or dried food because we knew we weren't going to find fresh things any more. Max found cans of something that looked like dog food, but it was for people.

'It's meat substitute,' said Billy.

'Has it got dead horses in it?' Max said.

'No. No horses, dead or alive, no donkeys, no sheep, nothing with four legs or even two legs. Only legless things go in this stuff,' said Billy. He squinted his eyes up and tried to read the small writing on the side of the tin. 'It's made out of nuts and . . . other things that are good for you.'

'Have you ever eaten dog food?' asked Max.

'Not yet.'

'Might you?'

'You never know,' said Billy.

We took as much as we could find from the supermarket. We even had to undo the expansion zipper on my suitcase to fit everything in. We'd never done that before. It felt like we had to because that's what everyone else was doing, but it still didn't seem right.

'It's for emergencies,' Billy said, like I'd accused him of something, only I hadn't said a word.

'What sort of emergencies?' Max's possum eyes were shining and he twisted his hands together.

Billy shrugged. Then he said, 'Visitors. You never know when we might have visitors.'

It was a long walk back to Dreamland. Max got tired and we stopped to have a rest. Max and me sat on the footpath while Billy picked some oranges off a tree that was leaning over the fence from someone's backyard. He filled up his pockets and his backpack.

'Don't the people in that house want their oranges?' said Max.

Billy sat down next to us and took his pocketknife out. 'There's no one living there.' He peeled the skin off the orange carefully in one long strip. It made me think about the competitions me and Dad had, using Minties wrappers. We used to see who could tear the paper into the longest strip without breaking it.

Billy gave the peeled orange to Max and handed his knife to me. It felt warm in my hand.

'Want to have a go, Skip?'

The handle was made from mother-of-pearl. I held a rainbow in my hand. Billy showed me how to hold it so I wouldn't cut myself.

'How do you know nobody lives there?' said Max. His face was dripping with juice.

'There's no one in any of these places; they've all been evacuated.'

'What's evacuated?'

'They've told everyone to leave.'

'How do you know?' I asked Billy.

'Albert Park said so.'

I wiped my hands on my pants. The bird started flapping inside me.

'It's No-Man's-Land. A bit of land in a war zone, where no one's supposed to be.'

'How come we're here, then? Why didn't you take us north like the others?'

Billy's hands knotted up. 'Why should I?' His voice went cold and hard. 'I never had anything before this all started. I've lived in No-Man's-Land for thirty years.'

I felt like I'd done something wrong, like I'd hurt Billy. He put his head down between his knees. I didn't know what to say. Billy got up after a while and put his backpack on. Then he started talking like he'd never left off.

'Besides, we've gotta wait till the lists go up.'

'What lists?' I'd almost forgotten.

'Red Cross, missing persons lists.'

Max's mother was a missing person. The bird folded its wings and I felt empty.

When we got back to the House of Horrors, Max and Billy started to unpack our provisions and I sneaked off to check on my books. I hadn't told the others where they were. I heard that in some places they torture you in a war. They drip water on you and shine lights in your eyes and burn you with cigarette butts, and they ask you questions until you tell them what they want to know. I didn't want Billy and Max to get tortured until they told where my stolen library books were. Sometimes when people get tortured they say things that aren't even true. Once, when I might have been eight or nine, some boys held my head down a toilet and flushed it until I said I loved Alex Winter, who is a boy. I only said that because I didn't want to get drowned. But I didn't think Billy or Max would tell a lie even if they were getting tortured.

After I knew the books were safe I went back to help the others. That's when we heard the baby again. I looked out of the two holes in the wall that were supposed to be a skeleton's eye sockets and I saw the girl. The baby's face was dark pink from crying, like the inside of a water-melon. I looked around at Billy and he looked at me and we both had 'what are we going to do?' looks on our faces. Then Billy got a tube of condensed milk that he'd found at the supermarket. He put it in his pocket and we went out our secret exit and over to the carousel. The girl had the baby up over her shoulder and was patting its back but it wouldn't stop crying.

Billy took the lid off the tube of sweet milk and held it out.

'Here,' he said, 'it's milk.'

The girl's eyes looked like purple flowers in her white face. She held the baby on her knees while Billy squeezed some thick, yellowish milk onto her little finger. Then she put it into the baby's open mouth. It was lovely when the crying stopped. Max got into the Chariot of Peace and sat down beside the girl, and after a while he reached out and gently touched the baby's tiny and perfect fingers.

'Little fingers, starfish fingers,' he said softly as if he was afraid even the sound of his words might hurt the baby. Then he touched his finger to the baby's nose. 'Little nose!' It was like Max had never seen a person smaller than himself. 'Can I give her some milk?'

'Got to have clean hands, Max,' said Billy. 'Babies have to have everything clean, else they get sick.'

We all watched the baby sucking and I hoped the girl had clean fingers.

After a while Billy said, 'Got a bottle for the little 'un?'

The girl didn't answer. She held out her finger for another squeeze of milk, and Billy gave her some. Then he passed the tube to me and got out his harmonica and started to play. After a bit the baby stopped sucking and went to sleep.

'What's her name?' asked Max and the girl looked at him and shrugged her shoulders. Then the lights came on in the hotel and she shivered and wrapped the baby up inside her red coat. She stepped down off the carousel. I saw the look on Max's face and I hoped he didn't ask her what I thought he was going to. A baby needs a proper home and a lot of other things that we couldn't give her and, besides, none of us knew how to look after a baby properly.

I gave the girl the tube of milk. I wished she didn't have to go out under the big teeth, but I didn't know if it was safe to tell her about the secret entrance. She took the milk and walked away into the night, and all we knew about her that we didn't know the night before was that she had eyes like pansies and skin like the moon.

That night I dreamt a skyful of stars but when I looked closer the velvet dark was filled with babies' fingers: tiny starfish hands opening and closing.

Next day the sun came out, red against the blue, like the rose in one of Salvador Dali's paintings. The hotel lights, No-Man's-Land and missing persons lists became distant things like the shark-fin ships and the ransacked city.

Even Billy seemed happier. He said there were things we needed to attend to.

'What things?' asked Max.

'Things to make life easier,' he said and he got a look of mystery on his face.

First we hung our blankets outside in the sun to dry because there were leaks in the tin roof of the House of Horrors. Then Max and me stacked our supplies up on the wooden framework inside the tunnel, because we hadn't got it all done the night before. It was like a shop. We put the cans on the bottom: alphabet soup because it was Max's favourite, tomato for Billy and me, peas, creamed rice, and a giant-sized can of fruit salad. Max and me arranged the jars from littlest to biggest: Vegemite, peanut butter and then pickled onions. The boxes and packets took up the most room: there was porridge and potato flakes, long-life milk, sugar, biscuits, noodles, muesli bars, dried fruit, matches and another tube of condensed milk. We hung the packet of marshmallows on a nail. I wondered how long the food would last us and if there would be anything left in the shops when we ran out.

Once we'd finished, Max and me went outside to see what Billy was doing. We couldn't see him but we heard noises coming from a tin shed that wasn't much bigger than a cupboard.

'We're in luck!' he said when he saw us at the door, and we went inside to see why. There were buckets and bits of wood and cans of paint and all kinds of tools in there. Billy had his coat off and he was doing something to the coffee-vendor's trolley.

'What are you making?' asked Max.

'A wigwam for a goose's bridle,' said Billy. That was what he always said when he didn't know the answer to something or he didn't want to tell you. Billy looked as if he knew exactly what he was making that morning, so I guessed he wanted to surprise us.

'What's a wigwam for a goose's bridle?' said Max.

Billy put a bunch of nails between his lips. He looked like a catfish. I think he did it so Max couldn't ask him any more questions.

'A wigwam, an Indian's tent, a tepee, a wigwam, wigwam, woo, woo, woo, woo, woo!' I drummed my fingers on my lips and made Indian sounds, and I danced out the door and into the wintry sun and Max followed me. We tore strips of rag off the flags on the dodgem cars and tied them around our foreheads. We threw our jumpers off and stuck our fingers in the mud and painted each other's faces and chests with ancient symbols of war and peace. Then we crept through Sideshow Alley where all the yellow ducks lay dying with bullet holes in their tin hearts. We were silent and stealthy and our arrows were swift and deadly as we tracked our mortal enemies through the dark. I could see Max's heart beating like butterfly wings under his skin and I knew he was scared, but he didn't cry because Indian braves never cry. We went outside to find our faithful steeds and then I saw the enemy, sitting on my pinto pony.

The girl in the red coat was back again.

11

The truest thing

The dancing girl wasn't really the enemy. I was glad she'd come again even though she was so pale and quiet and teenage. That was before I saw her dance. I didn't know that she was a bit like me on the inside except she had her dancing and I had my pictures.

Max and me covered up our ancient symbols with our jumpers when we saw her, and we went and told Billy she was back. He was screwing something to the coffee trolley.

'Is she?' he said. He didn't look at us but I got an idea in my head that the girl in the red coat was the visitor Billy had been expecting. 'Leave her be, she mightn't want company, yet.'

We looked at what Billy had made and I thought

maybe there really was such a thing as a wigwam for a goose's bridle.

'What is it, really?' asked Max.

Billy thought a bit before he answered. 'It's a multi-purpose kitchen appliance. See, you put your water in the sink bit and then you put your metal cover over the top of it and light your fire down here on the bottom shelf.'

Billy was like the handyman on Sam Kebab's television, showing us how everything worked. 'So you can warm things up on the top bit or cook over the coals down the bottom and, bingo! you've got your hot water for free! I thought I might take a sheet of plywood off the tunnel wall so we can use it from inside when it's raining.'

Billy's invention was brilliant, but it seemed like he was going to a lot of trouble if we weren't staying long.

'We'll leave it here for now, though,' he said, and I knew he was being careful because of the girl, even though by then she must have guessed we were staying somewhere close by.

'Is it lunchtime?' asked Max.

'If you can wait till I get a fire going, I'll warm your soup. There's a plastic bucket in the shed, Max, run and get it for me. You come with me, Skip.'

We crept under the platform at the back of the House of Horrors and went inside. Billy took another piece of mending wire from one of the carriages and then he passed me the big can of fruit salad and some alphabet soup and we went outside again. Inside the handle of Billy's pocketknife there was a nail file, a tiny pair of scissors, a screwdriver and an opener for tins that didn't have rings on them. He took the lid off the tins we'd brought outside.

'Pass me the bucket, Max,' he said, and he emptied the fruit salad into it. Then he poked a small hole in each side of the empty can, near the top, and threaded the wire through the holes to make a handle. 'There, now we've got a decent-sized saucepan to cook in.'

'Can I have some fruit salad while we're waiting?' asked Max.

'There's no rule against having seconds first,' said Billy. He always called dessert 'seconds'.

'Do babies like fruit salad?'

'Only when they've got teeth, Max,' said Billy.

'Don't they have any teeth when they're born?'

'No, they have to grow them.'

'Huh! What do they eat, then?'

'Milk. They just drink milk.'

'Boring!' said Max.

Billy lit the fire and Max got a takeaway coffee cup and

a plastic spoon and helped himself to some fruit salad.

'Are these real cherries, Skip?' he asked.

'It says so on the tin.'

We emptied the alphabet soup into the fruit-salad-tin saucepan and then put in some water. When it was warm we sat in the sun behind the tunnel and ate it out of foam coffee cups. Max tried to get all the Ms out first, but it was hard to catch them. We had two cups of soup each, and there was still some left over.

'Want a bit more, Skip?' Billy asked.

I shook my head. 'I'm full.'

Max was full too, and so was Billy. He tipped the rest of the soup into a cup and put the lid on.

'See if the girl wants it,' he said and gave it to me. 'Better wash that war paint off your face first; might scare the baby.'

Max came with me.

'We've brought you some soup.' I held the cup out.

'It's alphabet,' said Max.

The girl slid down from the pinto, took the baby out from underneath her coat and laid it on the seat in the Roman Carriage of War. Then she took the cup from my hands and sat down next to the baby. It was wrapped up in a blanket with blue dinosaurs on it, so you couldn't see its starfish hands, only its face. It looked like one of the cherubs carved on the carousel, except it was sleeping. I wondered if babies dreamt and what they dreamt about. Max got into the carriage and sat opposite the baby, then I got in and sat next to Max. The girl sipped her soup and didn't look at us. She said, 'Where's the old man?'

'He's around,' I said.

'You live here?'

'No.' Max looked at me and I felt my face get hot, even though it wasn't really a lie.

'Are you the baby's mother?' said Max.

The girl didn't answer. She took another sip of her alphabet soup and then another one until it was all gone. Then she leant back against the chariot and folded herself and the baby into her coat, closed her dark eyes and shut us out.

We went inside. Max and me drew on butchers' paper and then I showed him how to fold it to make cranes, which are birds, not machines, and they're supposed to bring good luck. When I looked out of the skeleton's eyes again, the girl and the baby were gone, so Max and me helped Billy take a panel off the back of the House of Horrors and put his new invention in place. Then he lit the fire, and that night we washed ourselves with hot water and soap and dried ourselves by the coals. When Max and me went to bed, Billy blew into his harmonica. He played all the places he'd ever been, all the sights he'd ever seen, the people he'd loved and the ones he hadn't. He played the blue times, the red, the yellow and the black.

You might think what I tell you next is all a dream, or that I've imagined it. I can't help it if that's what you think, but I swear it's true. Sometimes the truest things are the hardest to believe.

Maybe it was the moonlight leaking through the holes in the roof that woke me, or perhaps it was the music. In the part of me where memories are kept there's a small black box. I don't know how it got in there. It's just a plain, ordinary box and its corners are worn smooth. But when I look inside I see that it's lined with crumpled silk, I hear music that makes my heart ache, and a china ballerina in a pure white dress dances around and around and around. The music was playing in my head when I woke up.

I took Dad's overcoat off the nail and put it on. I felt in the pocket for my chalks, and stepped outside. Mist swirled between the deserted rides like tired old ghosts. I didn't hear the sounds of war, just sea sighs and the music that made my heart ache.

I was almost past the refreshment pavilion when I saw a movement from the corner of my eye. I stepped inside, into the shadows. Moonlight poured in through the broken roof and I saw the girl in the far corner of the room. She had her back to me and was taking her clothes off, layer after layer of the rags and tatters she carried around on her back like Billy and me did, because we had no place to leave them. Underneath everything else she wore something that looked like nothing, and fitted like her skin. She looked soft and newborn like a butterfly escaping its cocoon. I watched as she tied her cobweb hair away from her face and stepped up on a small wooden stage where she bowed herself down under the moonlight and raised herself up to the stars and stilled herself to listen to the music that only we could hear. Then she let the dance come out of her.

I'd never seen a person dance before, not in real life, not this kind of dancing. I didn't know how to look at it or what I was supposed to see. I searched for all the things I looked for in a painting: line, colour and movement, light and shade. This girl danced like light on water. After I'd watched for a while I looked with all of me, not just my eyes, and then I saw the meaning of the dance. I wanted to stop looking because it was so sad, but I couldn't because it was so beautiful.

Then the baby cried and the ballerina stopped and picked it up. I wasn't scared any longer. I came close and the girl looked at me and she must have known I'd seen the meaning of her dance because it was still shining in my eyes. I touched the baby's starfish hands and they were as cold as a merchild's. I drew flowers on the stage for the ballerina while she fed her baby something from a bottle. When I'd finished I reached out and touched her wrist and she let me wrap my fingers around her scars.

Sometimes words come out of me and I don't know where they come from or why. They're like falling stars tumbling through the universe; bright, burning things that can't be stopped. That's what happened when I looked into the ballerina's pansy eyes.

'Billy won't hurt you,' I said. I'd seen his fists and I'd heard his sharp words, but I'd felt his gentle hand around mine and I'd seen him cry for poor Bradley Clark. Now I understood that Billy was like my dad: that the only person he fought with was himself. 'He gets mad sometimes,' I told the girl, 'but he's like the mother and the father of Max and me and he's our best friend.'

I knew she'd been waiting for those words because afterwards she let me take her and the baby to Billy and to Max.

12

Song for Sixpence

A sixpence is a small and silver coin from the olden days. It's worth less than a shilling but more than a penny; it's worth six pennies. It was called 'sixpence' because 'pence' is short for 'pennies'.

Billy says an old sixpence is worth about the same as five new cents. He also says, 'No man is poor who has sixpence in his pocket.' That's a wise saying he made up all by himself. I know it's true, because now we've got Sixpence.

There's a song about a sixpence. It's a nursery rhyme that we learnt from Billy. He used to sing it to the baby who belonged to the dancing girl whose name was Tia. This is the way the song goes:

'I love sixpence, pretty little sixpence,
I love sixpence better than my life.
I spent a penny of it, I lent another of it,
I carried four pence home to my wife.'

Max knew another nursery rhyme about sixpence, but this was the one Billy liked best. We called Tia's baby Sixpence, because Billy used to sing the song to her all the time.

Tia said it was a stupid name, but she wouldn't tell us the baby's real name. In the beginning, I never heard her call the baby anything. She didn't talk to any of us much and sometimes she went away by herself and left Sixpence with us. To begin with I was scared we'd make a mistake, because we didn't know much about babies; Billy was an old man, Max was just a kid and I was somewhere in between.

Even though they can't talk, babies have a sort of secret language. You've got to figure out what their different kinds of crying mean. It seemed like Sixpence was always crying until we got better at telling what she wanted. We had to learn fast because of the sandbag wall.

In the mornings or late at night, when Max and me were sleeping, Billy would go down to the boardwalk. He'd meet travellers from the city on their way to someplace else and they'd swap information and share cigarettes. Billy sometimes told us things he'd found out from the travellers and sometimes he'd say nothing. One morning someone explained why the sandbag wall was being built.

'They're sending in peacekeepers,' he said.

'Does that mean the war's over?' I asked Billy. A thousand thoughts about what this would mean for us waited for me to pay them attention.

'No, they just come to make sure no one breaks the rules.'

'What rules?'

'Rules of war.'

I didn't know there were any rules of war. 'But it'll be good when they get here, won't it?'

'They're soldiers and they'll be armed. Keep well away from them. Don't go anywhere near them sandbags, do you hear?'

Billy's eyes got a wild look in them and his lips clammed up. I knew better than to ask any more questions. I wondered if we were already breaking one of the rules: the one about trespassing in No-Man's-Land.

The peacekeepers were why we started paying special attention to Sixpence. We couldn't let her cry too much.

Usually she wanted one of two things: milk or a nappy change. I didn't mind feeding her, but the nappy part was disgusting. I tried to get out of it, but Billy said we had to take turns.

Babies need a lot of things we didn't have, so Billy, Max and me went looking for a charity bin. Tia didn't want to come. The first bin we found was so full I couldn't get inside the slot. The next one was a lot further away, but it was only half full. I stood on Billy's back and pulled myself in. It was a soft landing but it was difficult to sort through all the clothes while I was in there.

'Just chuck things out,' Billy shouted. 'We'll look at them out here.'

We got a few thin towels and baby clothes, but Billy pounced on some old sheets. 'That's what we need!' he said. 'We'll rip them up and make nappies. Now let's see if we can find some milk powder.'

We walked to the supermarket we'd been to last time, but there'd been a fire. The shop was an empty shell, except for the melted metal shelves and burnt-out fridges. Billy didn't say anything; there was no need to – anyone could see it would be useless going in. We walked for a long time till at last there were shops ahead: a chemist, a post office, and a fish-and-chip shop with clouds of thick black smoke pouring from the footpath outside. A bunch of guys were setting plastic chairs on fire and hurling them across the road like fireballs.

'Why do they make things worse than they already are?' The words came out before I could stop them.

'It's the war,' Billy said. 'Makes heroes of some, cowards of others.' Sometimes his answers only left you with more questions.

He took us on a detour before we got too close to the fish-and-chip shop. We ended up around the back and sat behind a row of wheelie bins, eating oranges until it was safe to come out. The post office and the chemist shop had metal bars on the front windows, but round the back the high-up windows to the toilets had none; just narrow glass louvres.

Billy stepped up on a sewer pipe that jutted out of the wall, but he couldn't reach the window. I pulled a wheelie bin across, climbed up and jiggled the top piece of window glass until it came loose, then I lifted it out. The next piece came out easy, but the bottom one was jammed tight. Billy was too big to fit through. Max would have been the perfect size, only he was too short to step down onto the toilet when he got inside. It was up to me. I took all the clothes off my top half, because it was going to be a tight squeeze. Billy hung the torch strap around my neck and told me what to look for.

'I think it's called Infant Formula,' he said. 'It'll be in a big tin.'

I had to go in backwards. It was easy till I got to my shoulders, then it felt like my skin was scraping off on the metal window frame. I was scared the bottom piece of glass would break, but it didn't.

It was a goldmine in there. I found the milk and heaps of other stuff for Sixpence: spare baby bottles, soap and powder especially for babies, disposable nappies and even pink singlets. I stood up on the toilet seat and passed them all out to Billy.

'There's little tins of baby food, too,' I whispered out the window.

'She's too young for that,' Billy said.

'But when she gets teeth she'll need some,' I heard Max say, and I could tell he really wanted me to get some of those tiny tins.

'Just a few then,' said Billy.

When we got back, Tia and Sixpence had gone.

'She won't be far away,' Billy said. But I ran everywhere, looking. I was afraid we'd never see them again. Then I remembered the refreshment pavilion. As I ran towards it I heard Tia's voice coming from inside. I stopped to listen and heard her singing.

'I love Sixpence, pretty little Sixpence,
I love Sixpence better than my life.'

That's all she sang, just the first two lines. To begin with I felt happy; Tia did love her baby, I thought. But then she kept on, singing the same two lines over and over, and the longer she sang the more it sounded like the words came from some dark, empty place inside her. Some people, like my dad, have invisible scars; others, like Tia, have scars you can see. I was afraid Tia might be like Vincent who had both kinds of damage. It's a difficult job to look after a person who's damaged on the inside. Sometimes they won't let you. I felt lonely and wished I was six, like Max, and someone would take care of me.

I went inside and put Dad's coat on.

'Where are you going?' said Max.

'Just out.'

'Can I come?'

'No.'

'Don't be mean!' He stamped his foot and started to cry.

'Skip?'

I left before Billy had a chance to say any more. I felt in my pocket for chalk as I walked along the boardwalk. I should be practising. I should be reading my books, I should be getting an education. I didn't want to look after Sixpence and Tia and Max. The chalk snapped in my fingers and I threw it as far as I could. Soon it would be dark and the travellers would come along the boardwalk, like a flock of birds migrating to a place where they could survive the winter. I thought of waiting till they came and going with them, but I remembered what Billy said about heroes and cowards. I knew I wasn't a hero, but I didn't want to be a coward, so I went back inside.

Tia was there with Billy and Max. The coals under Billy's multipurpose appliance were hot and they were washing Sixpence in the red bucket with warm water and her special baby soap. After they dried her and sprinkled her with powder they dressed her in a pink singlet and a disposable nappy with pictures of giraffes on it. She smelt beautiful and I loved her with all my heart and soul. I wanted Tia to feel the same. Maybe if the empty space inside her was filled with love there'd be no room for sad and dark things.

Between us, Max and me made forty-seven paper cranes. Billy threaded them all onto bits of string and hung them up in the tunnel so Sixpence could look at them when it was too cold to go outside. On days when it was fine we packed the bottom of my suitcase with newspaper and put

Sixpence in on top. We zipped the case up until just her head was poking out. We put socks on her starfish fingers and a tea-cosy hat on her head and wheeled her down the boardwalk so she could see the seagulls flying free.

A sixpence is a small thing and so is a baby. I have especially made this chapter short because it's mostly about small and precious things, like sixpences and babies.

13

Ambushed

One day, when Tia didn't want to hang around with us, me and Max took our slingshots that Billy helped us make out of bike-tube rubber and forked sticks, and we went along the boardwalk to the information booth. There were two huge pots there, full of dirt and dead plants and cigarette butts. We scraped handfuls of pebbles off the top and put them in our pockets for ammunition.

When we got as far as the house next door to the orange tree I saw some pickets had come loose from the back fence.

'Look Max!' I whispered, even though we were at least five blocks away from the sandbag wall. 'Let's take a short cut through the jungle.'

I went first, squeezing through the gap in the fence and crawling through the bushes, when a crazy screech ripped through the silence. I was sure we'd been ambushed. We didn't have time to get our slingshots out. We dived for the ground, covering our heads with our arms. Air and dust gusted all around. I imagined a helicopter hovering above us, full of soldiers with guns aimed at Max and me. Maybe it was the peacekeepers. Then suddenly I figured out what the sounds were and I opened my eyes. It looked like an explosion in a pillow factory: feathers floated everywhere. We'd broken in to a chicken run.

Max and me rolled around among the feathers and dirt and straw, with our fists stuffed in our mouths. But the laughing leaked out of us; we just couldn't stop it.

'C'mon, let's get out of here!' I said at last, but Max had spotted a nesting box with heaps of eggs in it.

'I wonder if they're any good?' I said.

We threw six at the fence to test them out: three each. The shells smashed and the insides dribbled down the grey palings. Two of them smelt disgusting and four didn't. Even a person who's dumb at maths knows that's pretty good odds.

'Let's take some back to Billy.'

'What if they break in our bags?'

'They won't if we put this in with them,' I said and we gathered up handfuls of straw and stuffed it in Max's bag so the eggs couldn't move around as much. We packed twenty eggs in there and then we went next door to get oranges. We took our slingshots out and fired stones at them, but we couldn't knock them down, so I climbed up the tree and threw the fruit to Max. I saw an old rainwater tank turned on its side with a lot of sawn-up wood in it, and I made a mental note to tell Billy.

I wanted to run back to Dreamland, to show Billy what we'd found, but we had to be careful because of the eggs. When we got back Tia was there with Sixpence and we told them all about the chickens and the eggs and the dry sawn wood in the rainwater tank. Billy scrambled some of the eggs in the fruit salad tin for our dinner and we only had to throw four away.

After Sixpence had her bottle and her bath and went to sleep, Tia went outside. I wondered where she was going. It wasn't only when we couldn't see her that she left us; sometimes even when she was sitting right next to us it was like she wasn't really there at all. You could even talk to her and she wouldn't hear you. She reminded me of the sea; the way she came dancing towards you, wild and beautiful, and just when she was almost close enough to touch she'd rush away again.

Max and me had started drawing when I saw Billy leave. I knew where he'd be going. Max had given up drawing animals. He drew people instead. None of them had faces or bellybuttons, but they all had machine guns. I'd got so used to seeing them in his pictures that I didn't notice them any more. It was the same with the sounds of war. They'd become normal, like gulls calling and waves crashing, the blue notes of Billy's Hohner and Sixpence crying for her bottle in the night. So I should have been ready for what came next. I'd known all along it was pretty sure to happen but I still got a shock when I found out it had. Billy dropped the bombshell when he came back from the boardwalk.

'The Red Cross have got their list of missing persons up,' he said. 'It's time we found out if Max Montgomery is on it.'

Max's mouth gathered up into a circle like a button-hole. 'When?' he said.

I watched his face to see if that was what he wanted. But torchlight beamed back from his glasses and I couldn't see his eyes, so it was hard to tell. Billy says your eyes are the windows of your soul. He also says different coloured eyes are the sign of a good soul and that being able to see two sides of everything is a rare gift. I don't know if he just made that up, but I knew it was going to be hard to see the good side of losing Max.

'We'll leave in a few days,' Billy said.

I don't know if I believed that Max's mother might still be alive, but I knew it was only fair to give Max a chance to find out. And if she was alive it was only fair to Mrs Montgomery, because I was sure she wouldn't have deserted Max on purpose. She would have planned to come back for him the way she always had, with a smile and a hug and fish fingers for his dinner. It was just that she hadn't counted on the war.

I was glad we didn't have to leave straight away. You need time to get yourself ready when there's something difficult you have to do. Giving Max back to his mother was going to be one of the most difficult things I'd ever done.

Max had some getting-ready of his own to do. He was only a little boy, but I think he'd figured out that he might never see Billy and me again. Maybe another reason why he hadn't pestered us about going back to the city was because he was so certain his mother would be there waiting for him, no matter when we got there. I thought it must be nice to trust someone that much.

It was weird how Max and me spent more time by ourselves once we finally knew that we were going back to find

Mrs Montgomery. Max stayed inside more. He cut a lot of pictures out of a magazine we'd found in the coffee-vendor's trolley, and pasted them in his Book of After-school Activities. I didn't ask to look because he always showed me things if he wanted me to see them. The other weird thing was how Tia stayed around more, at least in the daytime. I got a feeling she guessed how much I dreaded losing Max. I had to use all my different techniques to go to sleep, and even then I'd wake up again. One night I dreamt that Max was wandering around in the city all by himself. I was sweating when I woke up. I looked at Max sleeping beside me and then I got up to find a drink. That's when Tia came creeping in through the secret entrance.

'What's up, Skipper?' she whispered. Tia was the only one who called me Skipper.

'Just thirsty.'

She brushed past me on the platform on her way to check on Sixpence. She smelt of stale scent and smoke and other night smells that I didn't know the name of.

'You feel hot,' she said. 'You're not sick?'

I shook my head. I didn't want to talk about the dream.

Tia took my hand. 'Come in with me and Sixpence for a bit,' she whispered.

'Where do you go?' In the dark it seemed okay to ask her. I felt her shrug. 'Tell me,' I said. 'I won't tell Billy, honest.'

'Up on the hill,' she said after a while.

'Where on the hill?' I asked and I felt cold all of a sudden because I knew what the answer was going to be. 'To the soldiers?'

She didn't answer.

'Why, Tia, why do you go there?'

'I get lonely.'

'But you've got me and Max and Billy.'

'Don't tell Billy . . . please, Skip. You promised.'

'But why do you go there?'

'I told you, I get lonely.'

'What do they do, do they talk to you?'

'Yeah, we talk.'

'I don't get it. You don't have to go up there. You've got Max and Billy and me to talk to; we're your friends. And anyway you shouldn't go up there. Do you even know whose side they're on?' I felt hot again. I wanted another drink. Maybe I was getting sick.

'They're just guys,' she said. 'I don't care whose side they're on. Maybe they're not on anyone's side.'

I sat up. 'Are they peacekeepers?'

'Peacekeepers? You've got to be joking. I'm the one who keeps the peace.'

'What do you mean?'

'Nothing, just that I make them happy, that's all.'

'Tia,' I said and my mouth was so dry I could hardly get the words out, 'you don't talk about us, do you? You haven't told them about Max and Billy and me?'

'Of course not, Skipper. I wouldn't tell them about you, never, cross my heart.'

I wondered if she knew about torture.

She reached out and touched my face. Her hand was as cool as an angel's wing. I closed my fingers around her wrist and felt a narrow chain.

'What's this?' I asked and she snatched her arm away.

'What's wrong with you, haven't you ever seen a bracelet before?' she said.

I didn't answer. I didn't even ask where she got it. I didn't want to know.

'Sometimes they give me things,' she said. 'I dance for them and they give me stuff, that's all. It doesn't mean anything.'

I got out of the carriage to have another drink, and then I went back to the Devil's Lair with Max. I couldn't sleep. I wondered what would happen if the soldiers wanted more than dancing from Tia. What if they wanted information? Would she give it to them? Did they watch her to see which way she went when she left them? I had to find a way of keeping Tia away from them. I had to keep her safe. I had to keep us all safe.

14

The Guru of Noticing Details

If I'd thought about it a bit more I mightn't have gone off on my own. But in a way I didn't have a choice. When I woke up, everyone else was still asleep. Max was wound up in Dad's coat, so I left it there and tiptoed down to where my books were hidden. I put the one about Monet in my backpack. I wanted to be by myself for a little while, just to think about things the way I used to; important things like light and shade and the meanings of colour. I was tired of wondering how to keep Tia safe and of pretending it wasn't going to hurt too bad when I said goodbye to Max.

I climbed the Ferris wheel and sat on the top seat. Then I opened my book. I read how, in the beginning, some people thought Monet's paintings were rubbish because he painted in a different way to most other artists back then. But Monet kept on practising to make his work better and he went for a lot of trips to the sea to study light and colour. My favourite bit on that page was where it said, 'Monet was later recognised as a master of meticulous observation.' That means Monet was like the guru of noticing details, or so Billy says.

After I finished reading that page, I turned to the picture of *The Water-Lily Pond*, and I looked at it until I had a clear space inside my head. That's when I got the idea.

It was such a great idea that I never even thought about telling someone else what I was doing or where I was going. I put the book in my backpack. I had to take it with me, because if I'd gone inside I might have woken someone up and that would have spoiled the surprise.

First I went to the house with the chickens in the backyard, because Billy told me once that chickens let you pick them up at night without making a fuss. It was morning, but only just, so I figured they might still be a bit sleepy. I didn't know that chickens are early risers. The rooster had the best tail feathers. They were long and curved like a rainbow made out of shaggy black-and-green ribbons. We eyeballed each other, me and the rooster, but as soon as I made a move he took off and I could tell there was no way he was going to let me get my hands on his tail feathers. In the end I had to make do with the already-fallen-off ones I found on the ground.

After that I went to the chemist. There was no one out the front this time. I went around the back and pulled a bin across, the way we had the time before. Someone had smashed the bottom piece of glass so there was more room to get through, but there were still a few bits of glass sticking up in the frame like sharks' teeth. I tried to pull them out but I couldn't, so I put my jumper over them. Then I stuffed my shirt in the backpack and chucked it through the window before I climbed in. I didn't have Billy's torch this time so it was hard to see anything until I got close to the front window. But that was okay because the things I wanted were up there.

There was gold and there was silver. I went for the silver; silver like the moon, silver like a sixpence. I could have taken a heart or a star, but I chose a tiny padlock on a chain. Padlocks are used for keeping things safe, that's why I picked it. It came in a blue velvet box. Then I saw a glass cabinet full of bottles of perfume, but I couldn't undo the catch and it still seemed wrong to break things, even if there was a war. Light was flooding in the front window by then and I thought I'd better hurry in case the others were awake.

On the way to the back of the shop I got another can of milk powder for Sixpence. I stepped up on the toilet seat and pushed my backpack through the window, then I dropped the can of infant formula after it. I didn't notice that my jumper had got pushed through with the back-pack until I put my hands up on the window frame. I found a couple of clear spaces and balanced on my hands above the sharks' teeth while I squeezed my shoulders through the gap. I was seesawing half in and half out of the window when I saw them.

There were two of them and they were waiting for me. One had my jumper tied around his waist. They grabbed my arms, one each. My guts hit the glass and I heard myself scream as they dragged me through the window. Then I landed, face first, on the concrete path. They rolled me over and one of them put his foot on my chest. I guessed he'd be about Tia's age. He wasn't very tall but I could see his muscly arms because even though it was cold he was only wearing a singlet. I reckon he liked wearing it so people could admire his muscles.

'Watcha doin' on our turf?' he asked.

'Sorry,' I said, 'I didn't know –'

'Strip him,' said the other one who had his head shaved, and a black leather collar studded with silver spikes around his neck. It was the kind you'd put on a pit bull terrier if you had one; only this kid was more like a greyhound or a whippet, with his skinny body and long nose. It's hard to stop observing things even when you're in grave danger. I guess that's the way it was for Monet, when he was practising to become the Guru of Noticing Details.

'See if he's got anything in his pockets,' said Greyhound Boy when he figured out I wasn't wearing much they could strip.

'I just came for the milk powder,' I lied. 'I've got a baby to look after.'

'A baby? You've got a baby? Bullshit you've got a baby!'

'It's true,' I said. 'Her name's Sixpence.'

'Sixpence! Yeah right, as if anyone's gonna give a kid a name like that. Let's see what else you've nicked.' He pulled my shirt out of the backpack.

I tried to get up, but the one with his foot on my chest took his other foot off the ground and let his full weight press down on my ribs. I could hardly breathe. Jags of glass buried themselves in my guts and I bit down hard, so I wouldn't scream.

'Anything else in the bag?'

'Just a book.' Greyhound Boy shook the bag and the Monet book fell onto the ground. The cover bent back like broken wings and the beautiful shiny pages fanned open.

'Don't!'

'What?' said the boy with muscles.

'Be careful,' I said. 'It's not mine.'

Greyhound Boy picked it up.

'Let him up, Pratt,' he said.

Muscle Boy took his foot off my chest. 'What's it about?'

'Monet. He was an artist.' I pulled myself up and leant against the wall. I could feel the blood running out of my nose and I tried not to look down at my torn chest and stomach.

'Yeah? What sort of pictures did he paint?'

For a minute I thought Greyhound Boy seemed interested.

'He was an impressionist. There's pictures in the book.'

'He's got stuff in his pockets, Zombie,' said the one called Pratt.

Zombies are the walking dead. Greyhound Boy sure had a nerve saying that about Sixpence's name.

'Don't just tell me about it,' said Zombie.

I felt Pratt's hand slide inside my pocket and pull out the blue velvet box. 'I s'pose this is for the baby too?' He waved it under my nose.

I didn't say anything.

'You've been lying to me, haven't ya, kid?' said Zombie. 'Said you only took the milk, said it was for a baby. Well, there's two things I don't like about you: you're a liar and a thief.'

He came really close. I think he would have grabbed me by the shirt like they do in the movies only I didn't have one on. I tried to concentrate on details so I wouldn't get scared. I noticed he had blackheads next to his nose. I've never seen a dog with blackheads. Zombie sucked hard on a cigarette end that was only about as big as my little toe, then he blew smoke in my face.

'I think I'll have to teach you a lesson,' he said. 'But first we'll have a competition. I'm gonna try and pick your favourite picture in the book.' He started turning the pages, making dirty fingerprints on the corners, but I didn't say anything.

'Is it this one?' he asked, showing a picture of a cathedral, a bit like St Mary's before the bomb fell on it.

I shook my head.

'Okay, so we can get rid of that one,' said Zombie. He talked slow and he smiled.

'No, please don't!' I said. But it was too late. He ripped the page from the book. A blade appeared from nowhere in Pratt's hand and I felt it press against my windpipe.

'Now,' said Zombie, 'let's see, could it be this one of a haystack?'

I shut my eyes.

Zombie ripped another page from top to bottom. Then he said, 'Tell you what, kid, I'm feeling generous. I'm gonna give you somethin' to remember me by. You can take the milk, whatever it's for, and give him back the bling, Pratt.'

I felt the blue velvet box in my hands. I couldn't believe I was getting off so lightly.

'But just to remind you not to come back on our patch again . . .' He flicked a cigarette lighter and held the flame to the bottom of my beautiful book. I shut my eyes and tried to remember all the things I'd read in it, all the pictures I'd seen, all the small details.

'Watch and learn, kid,' Zombie said.

Pratt grabbed a handful of my hair and yanked my head up.

'Open your eyes,' he hissed and I felt his blade press harder. The pages blackened and curled, then burst into flames. Flakes of burnt paper drifted away like small grey moths.

'Don't let there be a next time or it will be worse, much worse,' Zombie said.

Pratt shoved me forward.

I stuffed my shirt into my backpack and grabbed the infant formula. I didn't want them to know where I came from so I walked in the opposite direction. As soon as I was out of sight I ran until I was sure they weren't following me, then I stopped and put my shirt on, and the can of milk and the blue velvet box in my backpack. I checked in the side pocket to make sure the rooster's feathers were still there, and then I ran again, all the way back to Dreamland.

When I went inside, Billy, Max and Sixpence weren't there and Tia was still asleep, wrapped up in her red coat. I was glad because I was shaking and tired and there were things I didn't want to think about and questions I didn't want to answer. I put the blue velvet box in my pocket and climbed into an empty carriage. I'd got the two things I went looking for – something to send Max on his way and something to keep Tia with us – and that was all that mattered. I crawled under Dad's coat and went to sleep without even trying.

It was the screaming that woke me up. I opened my eyes and saw Max pointing at me.

Then Billy burst in. 'What's the matter?'

'There's blood all over Skip!' screamed Max.

I looked down to make sure Dad's coat hadn't slipped off and then I remembered about my nose.

Sixpence started crying and then Tia woke up.

'My God, what happened, Skipper?'

'It's all right,' I said, 'I just had a blood nose.'

Billy brought some water in a bucket, and a piece of rag, and started to clean me up.

'How did this happen?'

I never lied to Billy, but I couldn't say anything about the presents, and I didn't want to talk about Zombie and Pratt in front of Tia and Max. Before, it was only the soldiers we had to worry about, now things were different. We were getting squeezed in from all sides.

'I went back to the chemist shop to get another tin of milk for Sixpence. It happened when I was climbing out again. I fell down on the concrete.'

'But we've still got nearly a whole tin,' Billy said. He had his hand under my chin.

It's hard to act normal and calm when you're not telling the whole story and someone's looking at you very close and you're feeling like everything inside you has turned to jelly. What I really felt like doing was putting my head on Billy's shoulder and crying, except I was too old for that.

'I know, but it's getting harder to find things. I thought it would be a good idea to get a spare one . . .'

'You must've left early.'

'I couldn't sleep. I thought I'd be back before you were awake. I forgot how long it takes to get there.'

'Don't ever go by yourself again,' Billy said. 'Okay?'

'Okay,' I said. But, if it meant keeping my friends safe, I knew I'd watch while every single one of my books got burnt, and I'd let them scrape the last bit of skin off me. Only I couldn't tell Billy that, because of the soldiers on the hill and the promise I'd made to Tia.

15

Sharks' Teeth
and Honey

I slept for hours after Billy cleaned the blood off my face.
I could hardly move when I woke up; my head ached and
my stomach was glued to my shirt. I was almost glad no
one else was there, but I worried whenever Billy and Max
were away from me. I pulled a jumper on over my shirt
and went down to the beach, looking for them. We went
there often during the day because we couldn't be seen
from the hotel.

Max and Tia were playing hopscotch on the sand and
Billy was making castles for Sixpence. She was learning
how to sit up, but every now and then she'd lose her
balance and fall backwards. Then she'd lie there looking
up at the sky like she'd meant to do it all along.

Max ran across the sand when he saw me. He stared at my nose. It felt as big as a rhino's horn. 'Will it go back to normal?'

'I hope so.'

'Let's make a mermaid.'

She had seaweed hair and a Mona Lisa smile. Then the others went looking in the tidal pools for winkles to decorate her tail. I walked out and sat on the jetty, thinking about the present I was going to make for Max later on. I didn't hear Billy come. He sat down beside me and didn't say anything for a while. I felt a bit nervous, thinking he might be going to ask me more about that morning, so I got in first. 'When are we taking Max back?'

Billy cleared his throat and I knew something was wrong.

'I've been thinking . . . might be best if just me and Max go.'

I stared at him.

'I mean . . . I know you're pretty close to the little fella . . . it won't be easy . . .'

I couldn't speak. Billy didn't know my mother dumped me. He didn't know Dad wanted to die more than he wanted to stay with me. I never told him about all the foster families, the beltings, the bullying and the loneliness. But after what we'd been through together, how could he think I was weak? How could he think I'd let Max down when he needed me most?

'Nothing's ever easy,' I wanted to shout. 'Nothing in this whole bloody universe!'

Billy was staring at the water. His lips were moving and I realised he was still talking to me. '. . . if something happened, if I couldn't come back, you'd be okay, Skip. You're a survivor.'

Then I knew what this was all about. I should have guessed. I pulled myself up on my feet. My head ached. My gut burned. The world spun.

'Liar!' I screamed. 'This has got nothing to do with Max and me. You don't want me around. You never have. And you're only taking Max to the Red Cross to get rid of him. His mother's dead. You know she is.'

Billy lumped himself to his feet and faced me. His skin was grey, everything about him was grey. He leant back against the wooden railing. 'You don't understand.'

'Yes I do. You'll go back to the city, dump Max with the Red Cross and I'll never see either of you again.'

'Might be better that way.'

'Better for who?'

I burned. I tasted blood. I wanted Billy to feel my pain. I was a boxer, jabbing at him with words, dancing away, trying to land a right hook, make him pay with a knockout blow. 'You tricked me. You said my pictures were good and I believed you. I pinched the books so I could get an education. I thought you cared. Why didn't you just tell me to get lost? Why wait till now?'

Billy was old. His words were slow coming. 'Thought I could do it, but I was wrong. I'm no good, Skip, you deserve better. I had a boy like you once . . .'

'Did you lie to him, too?'

Billy's knuckles went white. 'You know nothing, you little shit!'

'Did you walk out on him?'

Billy bounced off the ropes and grabbed me by the shoulders. I thought I was going to pass out. 'I did something wrong, way back. They took my boy off me and locked me up. Never saw him again, spent my life paying for one mistake. No one wants you when you've been inside.'

The others were coming, racing along the beach. I ran to the sea end of the jetty and dived into the water. When I surfaced, screaming with pain, I heard them shouting my name. I swam until my arms were useless, then I floated on my back. Tears rolled down my cheeks and dripped into the sea.

I waited until the others had gone before I swam back to land. Then I sat on the beach until I was numb. I had to go to the House of Horrors to get my coat. Billy was still there. He was making soup and Max was colouring in, and even Tia was there, feeding Sixpence. I didn't look at their faces; I couldn't. No one said anything and I wondered what Billy had told them. I put Dad's coat on and took my wet clothes outside, then I went and sat on the platform of the carousel.

After a while I got a feeling that someone was watching me, but I didn't look up. I didn't care, not even if it was a soldier. When I heard uneven footsteps I knew it was Billy. He stood there, touching-distance away. I looked at his odd shoes and his frayed pants, then I slowly looked up at his face.

He held his arms out. I couldn't believe it. All I had to do was walk into them.

I couldn't remember anyone hugging me like that before. I didn't think I pulled away, even though it hurt like crazy, but I must have, because Billy opened Dad's coat up and took a look. It was a mess in there: all puffy, purple and red around the cuts. Bits of skin hung off and pus and blood were oozing out like the inside of me had gone rotten.

'What did you cut it on?' he asked me.

'Broken glass.'

'Best thing you could've done, jumping in the sea,' he said. He was serious, but I started to laugh. I couldn't help it. Then I was crying and Billy wiped his eyes on his sleeve.

'Better get you inside,' he said.

Tia and Max looked up. Sixpence was sleeping.

'Tia, take Max outside for a bit,' Billy said. 'Don't go far.'

'C'mon, Maxi baby,' Tia said and I was surprised because she didn't usually like it when people told her what to do.

First Billy cleaned his pocketknife in boiling water.

'This might hurt a bit,' he said, 'but I've got to see if there's any glass left in there.'

I bit down hard on my back teeth. I felt like I was going to throw up, or pass out. I tried to imagine Tia's face when I gave her the necklace. When Billy finished, he showed me the glass in the bottom of the red bucket.

'Sharks' teeth in my guts,' I said, 'that's what it felt like.'

'Hope I got it all,' he said. He made me lie down and poured bottled water over the cuts. Then he got out a jar of honey he'd been saving until the war was over and we could buy crumpets. He warmed some of it and smoothed it carefully over the worst bits.

'Old remedy,' he said, 'old as the Pharaohs. Keeps the germs away.'

After that he tore strips from the old sheets we'd found in the charity bin, and wrapped them around me. I watched his careful hands and wondered why he hadn't already gone after what I said to him. I was nothing to him; just a homeless kid who somehow got mixed up in his life.

'So what are we gonna do now?' I said when I was all wrapped up like a mummy.

'Truce?' Billy stuck out his hand.

'Does this mean you're not gonna shoot through?'

'Never said I was going to, Skip. Thought about it, but not for the reasons you think.'

'Why, then?'

'S'pose I'm a coward.'

'What do you mean?'

'Every time I look at you, I think about my own boy and how I stuffed his life up. Don't want to do the same to you.'

It was the first time Billy had given me anything from that far inside himself and I felt like I owed him. I wanted to tell him about my dad; about the times he spent all his pension money on booze and smokes and then sent me down to the Salvation Army to ask for food vouchers. And the other times when he got mad and threw things and swore at me. I wanted Billy to know that my dad gave me to the Welfare people and even after that I never stopped loving him, but I couldn't say it.

'Do you think Max's mum might still be alive?'

'Just a chance. I wouldn't be taking him otherwise.'

'Can I come?'

'Do you still want to?'

I nodded, then I told him about Zombie and Pratt. I said it fast to get it over and done with because I didn't want to think about it any more.

We heard Max and Tia outside then. So Billy gave us the soup he'd made, and acted like the rest of that day had never happened. He talked about us all going to find Mrs Montgomery, as if that's what he'd always planned.

'We'll go back the way we came,' he said, 'but this time we'll travel light. Just a backpack each.' That meant no suitcase and no books.

'Your things will be all right here, Skip,' he said. 'No one in their right mind would bomb a fun park.'

I couldn't help thinking about St Mary's and the State Library and the neat, painted houses with their golden doorknockers and striped awnings, bulldozed into a massive bonfire to make plenty of parking space for tanks and trucks and other machinery. But I never said anything, because now I knew I couldn't protect my books even if I had them with me. Billy tried to make the trip sound like a big adventure.

'Before we go we'll have a slap-up meal,' he said.

Max asked him if we could have a bonfire on the beach.

'See what I can do,' Billy said, and I reminded him about the wood in the water tank.

That night Billy was busy getting ready for Max's farewell feast and the trip back to the city. The first thing he did was some more of his fancy wirework.

'What is it?' Max wanted to know.

'Give you three guesses,' said Billy.

'A toaster?'

'Nope!'

'I know . . . it's a tepee for the goose's bride!'

'A wigwam for a goose's bridle, Max,' I said.

'Nope, it's none of those things! Give up?' asked Billy. Max and me nodded.

'It's a chicken cooker!'

'But we haven't got a chicken,' I said.

I saw Max look at Billy and then Billy nodded. 'Yes, we have!' said Max. 'It's in the shed. Billy and me got it before. We put it in my backpack. We got a girl chicken, so she won't crow in the morning. Do you want to have a look at her? Can we, Billy? Can I take Skip and Tia to see her?'

Tia was feeding Sixpence, and I didn't really want to look at the chicken because I didn't think it would be a good idea to get too friendly with something you are going to eat, but I went with Max to make him happy. We shone the torch through the window of the shed and I agreed with him that the chicken had a lovely face, even though I wasn't sure she had a smile exactly like the Mona Lisa.

At last Max went to sleep and I got the rooster's feathers out of my backpack. I cut two long strips of butchers' paper and coloured them in red. Then I borrowed a black pencil out of Max's wooden pencil box and I drew pictures of caribou, buffalo and wolves on one of the strips.

Tia put Sixpence to bed and whispered over my shoulder, 'What are you making?'

'A surprise for Max.'

'Show me when I come back.'

I turned around. Billy was doing something to his back-pack with his pocketknife.

'Don't go,' I whispered. 'I've got something for you, too.'

'What is it?'

'A secret.'

'Can't you show it to me now?'

I wanted to go and get the blue velvet box right then,

but I couldn't. I had to wait for the perfect time. 'Not till Billy goes to bed.'

'Show me when I come back, then.'

'Don't go,' I said again.

'I'll be back soon.'

'Please don't, not tonight.'

After she'd gone I made myself concentrate on my drawings. I did the best ones I'd ever done. I didn't think about Tia dancing while I stuck the feathers on the back of the paper with Max's glue stick. I didn't think about what the soldiers were saying to Tia. I just made sure the spaces between the feathers were exactly right. Then I pasted the other strip of paper along the back to make it strong and I joined the two ends together. When I'd finished Max's surprise I hid it with my books and I took out the blue velvet box and looked at the silver padlock on the chain. All I had to do was wait for Tia to come back. I told myself I had to be like Max who believed with all his heart, because she had always come back before.

Tia slept late the next morning. She always did when she'd been away. All night I had kept the blue velvet box in my pocket in case she got back in time for the perfect moment. I looked at her sleeping and couldn't be angry because Tia didn't know I could give her what she wanted. I put her present in the secret hiding place with my books and Max's surprise. I thought the perfect moment might come that night. I didn't know it would take so long.

16

The Circle of Brotherhood

Everything seemed to take longer that morning because my chest and stomach were stiff and sore. I did all the usual things, like giving Sixpence a bath and feeding her, which I loved. Afterwards I cleaned her dirty nappy, which I hated, and I promised myself that once I gave Tia her present she wouldn't have any more late nights and I wouldn't have to clean any more dirty nappies.

In the afternoon I got started on the extra things we had to do for Max's farewell, like carting wood for the bonfire and keeping out of the way while Billy caught Mona. I should have taken Max down to the beach, but I didn't know we would still be able to hear the chicken squawking from inside the House of Horrors. Max stopped colouring in when he heard it.

'Sometimes tribal people kill animals or birds to offer as a sacrifice to their gods, Max,' I said.

'Why would they want to do that?'

'Well, it's like giving up something good in exchange for something better.'

'What sort of things?'

'Things like . . . protecting the other members of the tribe or getting plenty of rain, that kind of stuff.'

'But I thought Billy was killing Mona because we like to eat chicken.'

'He is.'

'Why did you tell me about that other stuff then?'

That made me laugh. I should have made it into a game, then Max wouldn't have asked any questions.

Just before dark, Billy showed us what he'd been doing to his backpack the night before.

'It's a baby carrier,' he said. 'I've seen people wearing them in the city. Not exactly the same, but something like it. Try it out. Put Sixpence in. See, that's where her legs go.'

He'd cut two holes in the bottom, one in each corner. When Sixpence was sitting inside the bag, all you could see of her was her legs sticking out the bottom and her chubby face looking over the top.

'She looks like a little turtle,' said Max.

'I'll take her tonight,' said Billy.

I helped him put the bag on over his chest.

'You're supposed to put it on his back, dummy!' Tia said in her smiling voice.

'It's better this way,' I said, 'because you can look at her whenever you want to.'

Tia's pansy eyes looked at me slowly, then she tweaked my swollen nose gently between her fingers and kissed Sixpence on her brand new hair and danced away down the boardwalk like a feather in a storm. The rest of us followed, walking down to the sea with our provisions in my suitcase.

Billy lit the bonfire and I helped him make a hole in the sand beside it. When the flames died down a bit, Billy scooped out some red-hot coals and put them in the hole.

First we made Salvation Soup in the fruit salad tin. That was easy. We mixed Vegemite with hot water and added a packet of dried vegetables; corn and carrot, onion and peas. When the vegetables swelled up we put in some stale bread rolls. It didn't matter that they were as hard as concrete because they went soft in the soup and made it thicker.

Billy had already cut the chicken down the middle so it was flat. He sprinkled it with salt and cooked it over the coals in the wire rack he'd made from mending wire. I tried not to think about Mona's lovely face, because we hadn't had meat for so long. Max and me got the drumsticks. Billy got a wing and the parson's nose, because that was his favourite bit. It's the part of the chicken where the tail feathers grow. Tia had breast meat and she found a small bone, shaped like a V.

'That's the wishbone,' Billy said. 'You're supposed to dry it out for a couple of weeks before you pull it.'

'I know,' said Max. 'Grandpa and me do it and I always get the biggest bit.'

'Two weeks is too long,' said Tia. 'Let's do it tonight.'

She sat on the sand with her legs crossed and she licked her fingers clean, slow and thoughtful, while we all watched. Then she held the wishbone in front of her, up against the inky sky. Her white hair streamed out like birds' wings beside her moon-kissed face. She looked like a goddess. I stared, hardly breathing, with longing to be the chosen one. Then she pointed the bone towards me.

'Skipper.' I saw pearls in her mouth and the velvet cushion of her tongue and I heard the magic words come out of her. 'Me and Skipper will break the bone.'

We joined ourselves together with unblinking eyes and a pinky finger each around the wishbone. Then we pulled apart with a sudden snap, and a tick of bone dangled from Tia's finger. She closed it away in the palm of her hand like a charm.

'Don't tell anyone your wish,' Max said.

Tia closed her eyes. I made a wish too. I wished that Tia would make the right wish and that it would come true.

After the wishing, Tia walked away on the wet and shining sand. The wind howled and the waves roared and her footprints disappeared behind her. She was gone too long. I should have gone with her and given her the silver necklace. The longer I had to wait, the stronger I imagined its power to be. Until Tia wore it, I was afraid something terrible might happen to her. Then I saw her coming back to us through a mist of salt spray, leaping and curling under the moon like the waves.

Sixpence slept and Billy cried while Tia danced. Then Max and me threaded pink and white marshmallows and chunks of tinned pineapple onto pieces of wire and toasted them over the coals.

'Better get some sleep now,' said Billy when we'd finished eating. 'Early start tomorrow.'

'Wait,' I said. 'There's something else.' I'd got ready to let Max go and now I had to do it. I drew a circle around myself.

'Max,' I said, 'take your beanie off and come out here. Stand in the circle with me.'

Max stepped in beside me. The wet sand mirrored the sky and we stood in a garden of stars.

'This is the Circle of Brotherhood,' I said to Max. 'A circle has no beginning and no end. That means that even when we are far away from each other we will still be brothers.'

We spat on our palms and did our secret handshake and then I undid the side pocket of my suitcase and took out the surprise. He gasped because it was so splendid. It was an Indian brave's headdress. I put it on his head and the rooster feathers fluttered under the moonlight while I said a silent prayer to Max's ancestors. I asked them to comfort him and whisper wise thoughts to him and guide his footsteps through the dust. Then I said the speech I had been practising in my head. I said it out loud so that everyone could hear.

'This is the headdress of the brave, Max Montgomery; wear it proudly because you are very brave.' Then I kissed Max because I loved him, and everyone I had ever loved before had gone away and I had never kissed them goodbye.

17

The blessing and the bomb

When I woke up next morning I felt the wrongness straight away. Sixpence was grizzling. I sat up and looked into the carriage called Hell's Teeth. Tia wasn't there. I got Sixpence and put her in with Max and me. It was a bit of a squeeze because I couldn't put her on my chest. Then Billy came. The cold followed him inside and I smelt the salt and smoke on him and knew he'd been down to meet the travellers. I let my eyes creep open as slow as clam shells, and watched him feeling in all his pockets and looking on the floor of the Vampire's Nest, where he slept, and on the platform where you wait for the ghost train that never comes, and I knew he'd lost something.

We didn't have many things to lose. When you're in a war or you're doing a runner or when your friend is going away, it's nice to have the same things in your pocket as you had yesterday. I closed my eyes hard and made a wish that Billy would find the thing he'd lost. That made me think about the wishbone and I wondered what Tia had asked for last night. I hoped it was the right thing.

Billy says everyone has light and dark inside them. When Tia's light shone it almost blinded everyone. I was thinking about the night before and how her dance had been so beautiful it made Billy cry, when Sixpence started to cough. Then Max woke up.

'Where's Tia?'

I shrugged. 'Gone,' I said like I didn't care.

Max put his finger out for Sixpence to hold. 'She'll be back,' he said and I knew he was thinking about his mother.

Billy fed Sixpence and dressed her and then we packed our things, but still Tia hadn't come. Max and me looked everywhere we could but we didn't find her. We told Billy and then we went down to the boardwalk and I drew some pictures, but they weren't as good as I usually did. I couldn't concentrate. I wanted Tia to come back. I'd got myself ready to let Max go, and I didn't want to have to do it all over again.

We waited. Trucks roared up and down the hill all day. Then the lights came on in the hotel. I was afraid then;

afraid for Tia and for all of us. I wondered if they'd made her tell about us. If she did, it was my fault because I hadn't given her the necklace. Maybe there was no right time. I should have just given it to her.

Then Billy said, 'Can't wait any longer, we'll have to go.'

'What about Sixpence?' Max and me both said at the same time. But we didn't say 'personal jinx', and we didn't do a high five the way you're meant to.

'We'll have to take her with us,' said Billy.

'What about Tia?' I said.

Billy ripped a piece of builders' foil off the inside of the shed and wrapped it around two bottles of warmed milk. Then he stuck them down the front of his jumper and buttoned his coat. 'She mightn't come back,' he said.

I hoped he didn't mean ever. 'Couldn't we wait till tomorrow?'

Billy looked to see where Max was and dropped his voice down low. 'We might have waited too long already. They dropped another bomb last night. A big one.'

He lifted Sixpence onto his back. Max put his brave's headdress on and we filled our pockets with stones. I held his hand when we got to the train tracks. We were heading towards the city where precision bombs flattened churches and libraries. I was going to give my best friend back to his mother. Billy had a baby who didn't belong to him. He hadn't found whatever he'd lost and none of us knew where Tia was. I felt the wrongness of all these things inside me like grit inside my shoe.

The wind howled like wild dogs along the electricity wires, and we looked every way trying to see more than the deep blue darkness. The cold bit into Billy's bad leg and made him limp even more than usual. Sometimes we thought we heard voices – whispering, singing, crying voices – as we walked between the high, graffiti-covered walls. Sixpence was coughing again, and when we got to the north spur Billy stopped. For a minute I thought he'd tricked us; that he was taking us to the refuge.

'Pull her hat down around her face,' he said.

I pulled the tea-cosy right down and put the hole for the handle around the front, so Sixpence could breathe. Max and me laughed. It was the first noise we'd made for ages, and it sounded good.

'Finished?' Billy asked.

'Yes,' said Max, 'you can just see her little nose sticking out.'

Billy started to sing as he walked:

'I love Sixpence, pretty little Sixpence,

I love Sixpence better than my life.'

Then he whistled a bit and I looked into the distance,

trying to see the fire in Albert's tunnel. They say that on a clear, dark night you can see a candle burning from fifty kilometres away.

'Are we nearly at Albert's place?' asked Max.

'Must be close,' said Billy.

'Let's guess how many cat-and-dogs, Max,' I said. Max didn't know that was how you counted seconds, I had to tell him. 'Every time you say cat-and-dog, that's one second,' I said. 'Like this: one cat-and-dog, two cat-and-dogs, three cat-and-dogs. See, that's three seconds. Guess how many to Albert's tunnel and then we'll count. I say it will be . . . seventy-seven cat-and-dogs. No, one hundred and eleven.' I picked a high number on purpose so Max would get a surprise when it was sooner.

'I can't count to that many,' Max said.

'Doesn't matter, I'll help you. What's your guess?'

'I say . . . twenty-six cat-and-dogs!'

I lost count a few times, but I got to two hundred and nineteen cat-and-dogs before we saw what was left of Albert's tunnel. It used to be a square tunnel, made out of concrete panels, but something had landed on it and smashed one of the walls, and the roof had slid down. Now the tunnel looked like a crooked 'A'. I didn't want to go in there, but we had to because Sixpence was crying. Her voice sounded thick and strange.

'She needs a drink,' Billy said. He switched on his torch and shone it around inside. In the corner, where part of the tunnel had caved in altogether, I saw a heap of rags. I thought it might be Albert, but Billy flashed his torch away before I got a proper look. Then he took his backpack off. He passed Sixpence to me. 'She's hot,' he said, feeling her forehead.

'Should I take her hat off?'

'No, just feed her while I get a fire going.'

He gave me a bottle and I crossed my legs and nursed Sixpence inside my coat the way Tia did. I had to be careful so it wouldn't hurt too much, but I needed to feel someone warm and alive next to me. It wasn't long before I started thinking about Tia. I wondered where she was and I hoped she had her red coat on and that she wasn't scared.

Once the fire was going, Billy and Max and me ate ginger biscuits and drank tea, then Billy took out his Hohner. I lay down beside Sixpence with our hearts touching. I didn't hear the strangers come. I saw their faces in the firelight and thought they were God's red children. On the wall behind them I saw my primitive drawings and Max's handprint and mine, together for always. I thought my prayers to Max's ancestors had been answered and they had come to comfort him and whisper wise thoughts and guide his footsteps through the dust. Then I saw their faces; they were pale as ash and their eyes were like black holes. They looked like the living dead: like zombies.

I heard Billy talking. He sounded peaceful and I saw him take the ginger biscuits from Max's bag and put the used teabags back into the water in the fruit salad tin. So I looked at the strangers through slits between my eyelids. There were two men, one old and one younger, a woman who might have been someone's mother, and a boy who looked a bit older than me. They had bags and bundles and I saw that they weren't really zombies; they were like us, God's pale children. But I knew Billy would have helped them no matter what colour they were.

'Many on the road?'

'More and more every day. We heard there's a refugee camp further north.'

'You'll go there?'

'If we can, Dad's getting on. He's not so good at walking now.'

Billy poured weak tea into foam takeaway cups and handed them around. Then the biscuits.

'Haven't got a smoke, have you?' he asked.

'I am Thomas,' said the old man, holding out a packet

of cigarettes. 'Old Thomas.' He put his arm around the younger man's shoulders. 'This is my son, Tommy.'

Billy took a cigarette; a whole one that hadn't been smoked before. He held it under his nose and smelt it from one end to the other, then he put it in a pocket inside his coat. 'Much obliged, Thomas, I'm Billy.'

The old man dunked his ginger biscuit and took a bite and then he said, 'You headed north?'

Billy shook his head. 'No. We're going back to the city.'

The woman's mouth fell open like a handbag with a broken latch. 'Oh you mustn't!' she said and darkness spilled out of her. 'You mustn't take the children there. It's not safe.'

I opened my eyes properly then and sat up.

'We're taking the little fella to find his mother,' said Billy.

The woman looked at Max who was sleeping beside me, wrapped up in a blanket.

'He's only six, he needs his mother.'

Then Sixpence coughed and woke up and I put the bottle in her mouth again. The woman looked at her red cheeks and felt her forehead, the way Billy had. 'She has the fever. She needs water, boiled water. Where is her mother?'

Billy shrugged. The woman didn't make a sound but I saw the tears rolling down her cheeks and Tommy put his arms around her and I felt suddenly afraid for Sixpence.

Billy took his Hohner out. Sometimes he could get Sixpence to go to sleep when he played. He picked a song he'd taught to Max and me. A man called Dylan wrote the music and the lyrics. Billy knew forty-seven of Dylan's songs. He said he loved them all, but the song he played in the Albert Park Hotel was a favourite of his. It was a song about trying to find answers. Billy said it reminded him of me, because I was so full of difficult questions that no one had answers for.

Old Thomas knew the words and he sang while Billy played. Sixpence went to sleep but when they finished the song, Old Thomas asked for another one, and they kept on going. The last one Billy played was the one he most often played for Max and me when we were going to sleep. He said the words were like a blessing and you wouldn't find a better one in any prayer book anywhere in the world. My favourite part of the blessing song is the bit about always knowing the truth and seeing the light that surrounds us. It's like he wrote that line especially for me. That's what Old Thomas was singing when the rest of the city got blown to smithereens.

When someone famous dies – like the president of the United States of America or Princess Diana or the Pope or Kurt Cobain, people say that years later they can still remember exactly what they were doing when they heard the news. When I'm as old as Old Thomas, I'll still remember the music Billy was playing when that bomb fell.

18

Chickening out

There's a line in the blessing song about being courageous and strong. Max was both those things on the night the bomb fell. He stood up with his brave's feather hat on and looked outside at the fireball that was once our city. Then he put his hand in mine and we followed Billy and the others out into the red and the black. He said nothing when we turned back the way we'd come from.

When we got to the place where the others were leaving us to go north, Old Thomas said, 'Come with us, Billy. Get the little ones out before it's too late.' His eyes went to the bump in my coat where Sixpence was sleeping. 'Sometimes it's better to live without a mother than not to live at all.'

I couldn't have blamed Billy if he'd given up on Tia, and now Sixpence was sick, things were even more complicated. His lumpy fingers wormed around each other while the rest of us waited for him to answer Old Thomas. I moved closer to him.

'We can't,' I said at last. 'We've gotta give Tia one last chance.'

'You could go with Thomas,' said Billy, 'you and Max.'

'What about you?'

'I couldn't make it that far.'

'And Sixpence?'

'I'll take her with me, in case Tia –'

'I'm coming with you.'

I saw Thomas look at Max. Billy saw him, too.

'No!' I shouted. 'Max stays with me. We're sticking together. We'll all go back for Tia.'

Billy said nothing. There was no fight left in him.

Old Thomas put his overnight bag down beside the steel rail and opened it. He felt around in the dark inside and found a small black box like the one I sometimes saw in my head. Old Thomas opened it and took out something that shone like treasure. Tommy put his hand on his father's sleeve and looked at him. 'Dad . . .' he said and the sound of it was hardly a sigh.

'I only went because I was sent,' Old Thomas said gently to his son. Then he looked at Max. 'May you always be brave and strong,' he said. The words were bits of the blessing song that were still floating around in our heads after everything else had got blown away. Old Thomas shook Max's hand as if Max was grown-up. Next he put a long striped ribbon around Max's neck. It hung all the way down to the top of Max's old-man trousers, and on the end of it was a golden medal.

'Take these,' Billy said and his voice sounded like he'd swallowed sandpaper. 'It's not much.' He gave Old Thomas the rest of our oranges. They looked nearly as beautiful as the golden medal, and Old Thomas said they were even better because you could eat them.

When we got back to Dreamland the sky was the colour of roses and violets and ash. It made me think of the bruises you get on your heart when you see things like a stranger giving a little boy a golden medal. Before that I thought war was only about taking things away, and I always thought of it in black and red.

We couldn't tell if it was day or night and we didn't care. We came through our secret entrance and didn't see the huge, dark shapes nosed in beside the Ferris wheel. Max climbed into the Devil's Lair and I got in beside him with Sixpence. I squeezed some sticky milk on my finger and let Sixpence suck it until we all fell asleep.

When I opened my eyes again, the forty-seven paper cranes were dancing and light flooded in through every crack and nail-hole. An ocean of noise swallowed me up and held me under. I flung myself out of the carriage, dragging Max with me, holding Sixpence close, running for the door, and then I saw Billy. He was standing still, looking through the skeleton's eyes. I pushed him out of the way. Outside was a tank, two trucks and a group of soldiers with guns hanging off their shoulders. I'd never been that close to a tank before. It was almost as big as the Carousel of War and Peace.

Sixpence started crying. Her breathing sounded like someone sucking the last bit of a thickshake through a straw. I pulled the tea-cosy off her head. Her hair was wet with sweat. 'Get me some water,' I shouted.

Billy came back with a screw-top bottle. I splashed some on Sixpence, to cool her down, and shoved the rest back in Billy's hands. 'Put the rest in her bottle.'

I'd made the wrong decision. Tia couldn't come back now. We should have gone north with Old Thomas and his family. Now we were stuck in No-Man's-Land with a sick baby. Sixpence needed clean water and maybe a doctor and medicine as well. But how do you get all these things when an armoured tank is parked almost at your door?

Max pulled at my sleeve, wanting to look. I shoved him away and held Sixpence tight against my chest while she drank. The pain was payback for all the wrong things I'd done. I sang to her while the soldiers talked and laughed and smoked, and climbed in and out of their war machines. No one could hear me. After a while the top part of the tank turned slowly until the barrel was pointed at the House of Horrors. Did they know about our hide-out? Had Tia told them? If I ran outside would they shoot me?

The engine revved louder and then the tank reversed slowly. A shout went up from the soldiers and then they cheered. I felt the fall of the Ferris wheel through the soles of my feet. The soldiers who were left behind, after the tank rumbled away, got in one of the trucks and drove up the winding hill to the hotel.

Sixpence went to sleep at last and I tucked her into the Devil's Lair. Billy lit the fire.

'Should we head north?' I said.

He didn't answer. I knew he wouldn't. I shouldn't have asked. It feels bad when someone asks you a question and you haven't got a clue what the answer is. But I was mad with myself for making the wrong decision and angry with Billy for forcing me into it.

No one else came near us for that morning. Billy lay down to rest his leg so, early in the afternoon, Max and me slipped outside. I told him we had to be as quiet as Indian braves stalking their prey, only this wasn't a game, it was for real. We tiptoed behind the House of Horrors and climbed, quiet as mice, into the back of the truck that was parked near the refreshment pavilion. There were metal drink containers and camouflage caps and back-packs with everything you could need inside them. There were fancy sleeping-bags called Feathersoft Microfibre, little gas burners to cook on, and tin plates and mugs. I started to feel better.

I decided to make a plan in my head the way I did when I was running away. Only this time I wasn't running away from anything or anyone: not the teachers who told me I was stupid because I couldn't do maths, or the people who belted me when they were supposed to be looking after me, or the ones who said my dad was crazy in the head because he could hear guns firing and people screaming ten years after he fought in someone else's war. I was going to a place where I would never have to run away again; somewhere I could get my education and put my hands up to the sky and see the way the light falls and where the shadows lie, a place where I could catch the wind and find answers to my difficult questions. I know that sentence is long and has too many joining words in it but sometimes, when I'm angry, words burst out of me like a shout, or, if I'm sad, they spill out of me like tears, and if I'm happy my words are like a song. If that happens it's one of my rules not to change them because they're coming out of my heart and not my head, and that's the way they're meant to be.

I wasn't going to let things happen to me any more. I was going to make them happen. I was making a plan; I was going and taking Billy with me, and Max and Sixpence. If Tia would come back I'd take her, too, and everything would be perfect.

'Max,' I said and happiness spilled out of my lips, 'how do you get to Gulliver's Meadows?'

When you are only six and you go for a ride in a car, you don't take notice of things like street names, or if you go by train you don't pay attention to the signs on stations. Even if you could read them, there are more interesting things to look at.

'You just go up to the corner and turn towards the airport.'

'Which corner, Max?'

'The one near my house.'

'What's your address?'

'One hundred and thirty Mount Alexander Road. Near the shop that sells beds. It's got a sign with a monkey under a doona.'

'What suburb?'

'I don't remember, but the monkey's got purple pyjamas on.'

Then I remembered something. 'Let's go inside,' I said to Max. 'Don't take anything yet or the enemy might get suspicious.'

Max looked longingly at the camouflage caps.

'Well, just a cap then. We'll get the rest of our supplies later.'

We stuffed the caps up our jumpers, climbed out of the truck and went inside. Billy had dozed off and Sixpence was still asleep. Her cheeks were red and her nose was runny, but when I touched her forehead I thought it was a bit cooler. Max and me crept past them and lay on the platform looking at the pictures in his After-school Activities book. We turned the pages until we got to the one of the cows, and I saw it was a photograph, just like I'd remembered.

There's a game Dad and me used to play where you put a lot of things on a tray and look at them for a while, then you cover them with a cloth and try to remember what's underneath. I used to beat Dad nearly every time. He said it was because I was observant. That was before I knew anything about the Guru of Noticing Details. I can still remember what Dad looked like, even though I haven't got a photo of him.

I looked at the photo of Max's grandpa's farm. I observed the way the long-stemmed grass leant over like the wind was blowing, and I noticed the small white post beside the road that was almost hidden in the grass. I looked at every single part of that photograph until I could remember it.

I forgot about how mad I'd been with Billy in the morning. I was bursting to tell him about all the things Max and me had found. I wanted to tell him about my plan and ask him if he could drive a truck.

The minute he opened his eyes I said, 'I've got a plan to get us outta here, Billy, and you won't have to walk!' I showed him the photo in Max's book. 'That's where we should go.'

Billy took the book in his hands and stared at the photo for a while. Then he said, 'Looks like it's somewhere in the country, Skip.'

'Yeah, it's Max's grandpa's farm.'

How do you plan to get there?'

'A truck.'

'An army truck?'

'Yeah. Can you drive?'

'Used to, way back. But there'd be roadblocks; they'd stop us.'

'There's army clothes in the back, Billy. Max and me found them. You could dress up. No one would know. We'll go at night.'

'We'd need ID. And what about keys?'

'You don't need keys. We saw it once on Sam Kebab's television, don't you remember? You just do something to the wires under the dashboard, and the motor starts.'

'Don't believe everything you see on the telly. Mightn't be as easy as you think.'

But Billy could do anything. He could make toasters out of mending wire, saucepans out of fruit tins, kitchen appliances out of coffee trolleys and baby carriers out of backpacks, so what was to stop him starting a truck without a key?

'That's all you gotta do. I've got the rest all worked out. Please Billy; I know you can do it!'

Billy wouldn't look at me. He picked at his broken fingernails and then stared at the cracks in the floor.

That's what Dad used to be like. He'd stop doing even the easiest things, like getting dressed, answering the phone or walking outside to the letterbox. When I'd ask him what was wrong, he'd lie and say 'nothing'. Then he'd stop talking to me. I hated that worst of all. I felt like it was my fault, somehow. Once I asked him why he wasn't talking to me and he screamed, 'Because I'm scared! Your old man's scared. Go to school and tell that to your mates!' Dad didn't know I had no friends.

'What are you scared of, Dad?'

'I don't know, that's the worst part of it, I'm just scared!'

Not long after that they said he couldn't take care of me. I told them I didn't need looking after. I tried to explain that they'd got it wrong, that it was me who looked after Dad, but they wouldn't listen. They said Dad needed 'professional help'. They told him it would be best if I went and lived with someone else for a while. They told me it was the best thing I could do for Dad.

It wasn't his fault. We both let go.

This time there was no one to help. I looked at Max. He was sitting there next to Billy with his eyes all wet behind his glasses and his medal on; Max who was too little to do anything useful except be brave. Then Sixpence woke up, crying, and I wondered if it would have been better if she'd never been born. She was sick, and her mother wasn't here because all she cared about was herself. And now Billy was chickening out on all of us.

I'd had enough of letting other people decide what was best for me. This time I wasn't going to get cheated out of all the things I dreamt of. Courage and strength go together in Dylan's blessing song, but it was anger that made me smash my fist through the wall of the House of Horrors. I shouted at the top of my voice, 'Well if you won't bloody well help me, I'll do it myself!'

19

Captain of our boat

I got into Hell's Teeth with Sixpence that night but I didn't do my visualisation technique because I needed to think about my difficult circumstances. Besides starting the truck without a key, I had to figure out how to get to Gulliver's Meadows. I needed a book of maps so I decided that when Billy went to sleep I'd sneak outside and see if I could find one in a truck. I heard the Vampire's Nest rattle, so I knew Billy had gone to bed, but I had to wait until he started snoring because sometimes he was like me and stayed awake for a long time. But trying to make plans is sometimes better than the visualisation technique for sending you to sleep.

I didn't hear Billy snoring and I didn't hear Tia come inside. When I opened my eyes she was sitting on the platform watching Sixpence sleep. I sat up and Tia stepped into Hell's Teeth, graceful as a poem, and laid herself down beside Sixpence. I looked at her moonskin face, her pansy eyes and her cobweb hair and I knew I would go on giving her one last chance for ever.

'We're going away, Tia,' I whispered.

'Where to?'

'The country.'

'What for?'

'I want to make a garden,' I said and I was surprised because I didn't know that was going to come out of me.

'A garden?'

'A garden with a lily pond. I want to see how light falls on water,' I explained.

'I've never seen a lily pond.'

'Me neither, except the one in Monet's garden, but I only saw that in a book.'

'How will you get there?'

'In a truck.'

'An army truck?'

'Come with us, Tia. Please, come with us.'

'Do you know which way to go, Skipper?'

'I'll get a map. There's got to be a map in one of the trucks.'

'Can you drive?'

'Billy can.'

'Billy's going, too?'

I didn't tell her Billy was afraid. Billy was my friend. You don't tell anyone things like that about your friends, even when you're mad at them.

'We're all going,' I said. 'Billy and Max and . . .'

'And Sixpence? You're taking Sixpence? Take her, Skipper, take her with you.'

'You'll come with us then?'

'Even if I don't, I want you to take her.'

'Come with us Tia. We came back for you, especially. You've gotta come.'

'Promise me you'll take Sixpence. You love her, Skipper; I know you do. Promise me, whatever happens, you'll take care of her.'

'You're her mother.'

'I'm only fifteen, Skipper.'

'So what, you're still her mother and she's sick.'

'You never told me that! What's wrong? Is she gonna be okay?'

'Sssh, don't wake her up. She's hot and her nose runs and it's hard for her to drink. What do you think's wrong?'

'How should I know? Fifteen's old enough to have a baby, but it's not old enough to be a mother.' She peeled back her sleeve, grabbed my hand and rubbed it over the inside of her wrist. 'See,' she hissed, 'I've got the scars to prove it!'

'You could learn,' I said.

'Think so?'

'Yeah, sure you could. Come with us, we'll help you.'

'Truth?'

We linked our pinkie fingers together.

'Truth,' I whispered.

'I'll come then. But if anything happens, promise you'll take care of Sixpence.'

'Nothing's gonna happen.'

'Just promise.'

I promised her. Then I said, 'I've got something for you.'

'What is it?'

'The surprise I told you about, remember?'

'Oh yeah,' she said. 'I do remember.'

I took the blue velvet box out of my pants and put it in Tia's hands.

'Oh, Skipper!' The silver chain trickled through her fingers like a waterfall. Then she looked at me with her eyebrows pulled together.

'I got it from the chemist,' I said, but I saw that wasn't what she wanted to know.

'It's for free,' I told her. 'I don't want you to give me anything. I just want you not to go with the soldiers.'

She put the necklace on.

'Thank you, Skipper,' she said. 'It's beautiful.'

I waited for her to say she wouldn't leave us again, but she didn't. I had to ask her. 'Promise me you won't go with the soldiers.'

'I don't make promises,' she said, 'in case I can't keep them. Sometimes you can't help it; things stop you.'

'I'll get you more stuff, if that's what you want,' I said.

'That's not what I want.' She leant over and kissed me on the mouth. I felt it go deep inside me with other things I'll never forget: like Dad waiting for me at the school gate, the birthday cake that had my name iced on top, and the china ballerina that was my mother's.

'That's for free, too, Skipper,' she said.

I didn't know what to say when someone's given you a small free kiss in the dark, so I asked her, 'Why do you call me Skipper?'

''Cause you're the captain of our boat,' she said, and we drifted off to sleep; Tia and me together, like praying hands, with Sixpence snug between us.

When I woke up Tia was gone and I thought I might have dreamt it all until I saw the book of maps beside me. I looked outside and it was still dark, so I made a fire and boiled water from the tap near the shed. I mixed up enough milk to last all day and I fed Sixpence and washed her in the bucket and gave her a fresh nappy and clean clothes. Her cheeks weren't as red but she only drank a little bit, and she cried after each suck, like the milk hurt her throat. I sat her in her pouch and put it on back-to-front, even though my chest and stomach still hurt. I wanted her near my heart because of the promise I'd made to her mother.

That morning I felt like I really was a captain. I had a plan and a book of maps and I was going to take care of Billy and Max and Sixpence, and Tia too, if she'd let me. I made a cup of sweet black tea and took it to the Vampire's Nest for Billy. Then I stuck the book of maps right under his nose.

'See,' I said, 'we are going. Tonight I'm gonna find out how to start the truck. Tia's coming too,' I said as though the words had power to bring her back to us.

Billy said nothing; he stayed in his carriage and drank his tea.

I spread the embers out and let them go cold. I washed my hands and squeezed some sweet milk onto my finger and gave it to Sixpence to suck while I tried to rock her to sleep.

Then I heard what I'd been expecting: the sound of a truck arriving outside. Through the skeleton's eyes I watched it pull in next to the one they left the night before. Soldiers jumped over the tailgate with guns swinging from their shoulders. I watched everything they did. They leant on the trucks and spat on the ground. One of them shot at a seagull with a pistol and the others laughed when it fell out of the sky. Only one didn't laugh. He had pimples, and his coat was way too big. He looked like a kid pretending to be something he wasn't, like Max and me sometimes did. He opened a truck door and climbed up into the driver's seat, but I couldn't tell if he'd used a key to get in. None of the soldiers seemed in a hurry to go.

It was like playing chess, where you're waiting for the other player to make a move before you can decide the best thing to do. Max and me got tired of waiting, so we looked at the book of maps and the photo of his grandpa's farm. We kept quiet and tried not to think about being hungry or what would happen if Sixpence woke up.

At last the soldiers roared off in one of the trucks. I waited until the sound faded away and then Max and me went outside, leaving Sixpence with Billy. We checked to see if any of the doors on the truck were open, but they were all locked. Then Max kept watch while I got in the back and had a good look at everything. I found a torch that worked, and bottled water, and silver packets with pictures of food on them. It was dried food. There was every kind you could think of: meat and vegetables and rice and even sweet things like chocolate pudding. I didn't know how you could have a flat chocolate pudding. There were tools, too: screwdrivers and spanners and other things in a metal box. I picked up the biggest spanner and felt the weight of it in my hands. It felt heavy enough to break a window.

'It's a goldmine, Max,' I said, and I stuffed heaps of silver packets down my jumper. 'Let's go back and show Billy.'

Some of the things had to be cooked but the dried meat was in sticks and you could eat it without doing anything to it. It was hard to chew, but yummy. Then we had dried fruit and nuts and something else that was supposed to be cheese.

'Eat as much as you want,' I told Max and Billy. 'There's plenty more.'

Once we were full I got the book of maps out again. I could tell Billy was watching me, even though he was pretending not to. After a while he sighed. 'Listen Skip,' he said, 'you don't even know where Max's grandfather lives. You haven't got an address or the name of the town or anything. How do you think you're going to find your way there?'

'Can I have a loan of your book?' I asked Max. He brought it over and I found the photograph of Gulliver's Meadows and showed it to Billy.

'We've been through all this. Gulliver's Meadows is just the name of the farm. You won't find it on any map,' he said.

'Yes, I know, but look.' I showed him the small white post almost hidden by the grass on the side of the road, and I pointed to the painted black numbers and letters. 'Maybe that's the highway number.'

Billy stared at the photo for a minute, then he looked up at me. 'You're right, Skip,' he said, 'it is, and the letter underneath is the nearest town and the number of kilometres from it!'

I saw a lick of fire in his eyes like someone had struck a match, and I was sure it wasn't too late to save him. Everything was starting to work out; once it was dark I'd smash one of the truck's windows, we'd get in and Billy would figure how to start it. My thoughts skipped ahead. I saw a lonely, white-haired old man, saw him wave and smile as we drove towards him. I saw him open the door of his home and welcome us inside.

But Billy still had doubts. 'Even if we did find the place, Max's grandpa mightn't be there,' he said. I didn't want to listen.

Then Max said, 'He isn't. It's Mummy's house now, only we don't live there, except in the holidays.'

'Where's your grandpa?' I said.

'He went to heaven last summer and Mummy said he's never coming back.'

20

The Third Side

I was shocked to find out that Max's grandpa was dead, but we had to get away from the city and I didn't know where else to go. I decided to stick to my plan. There wasn't much to take from the House of Horrors. I had my books and Dad's coat, and Max had his feather headdress and the medal Old Thomas had given him. We packed our blankets and bottles of milk for Sixpence. Everything else we needed was already in the truck. The only thing missing was Tia.

I looked out through the eye sockets towards the Boulevard Hotel. It was almost dark. Seagulls drifted like scraps of foil above the lights.

'Can you see her?' whispered Max.

I whispered, too, although there was no need. 'Not yet.'

I said it fast; I didn't want to talk while I was willing Tia to come. I visualised the shattered window, Billy's clever old hands under the dashboard, and I heard the engine roar. I imagined Max and me in the back of the truck with Tia and Sixpence, warm and safe in our Feathersoft Microfibre sleeping-bags, and Billy, in a soldier's cap and camouflage jacket, driving us through the night towards Gulliver's Meadows.

Sometimes, when I have bad thoughts, I make a noise inside my head. It fills my ears up, like when I'm under-water, and drowns the thoughts out. While I was waiting for Tia I got some bad thoughts, like: are there such things as soldiers with long grey whiskers? How much fuel is in the tank of the truck? What would we do if we got stopped at a roadblock? So I shut my eyes and made the noise. Max was pulling on my sleeve but I didn't pay him any attention because you have to concentrate to do the noise properly. Then I felt vibrations coming up through the soles of my feet and I knew I'd waited too long for Tia.

The House of Horrors shook as though the walls were made of cereal packets and light poured in through the cracks. The tank was back, followed by a truckload of soldiers.

Sixpence woke up and screamed with fright at the noise. I grabbed her out of the carriage and pressed her face against my chest to smother her cries. I shoved my free hand in my pocket and squeezed the tube. Milk went everywhere. Outside, the engines died and boots clattered on the concrete. Sixpence sucked in some air. I slid my finger in her mouth and she screamed again.

I had to do something or she'd get us all killed. I shoved her into Billy's arms and pushed him and Max towards our secret entrance. 'Get out, wait on the beach!'

The boots came closer.

I jumped off the platform and rolled underneath the wooden slats, pulling the suitcase after me. Strips of light fell through the cracks onto my face, and splashed over the walls.

'Ghosts!' I heard someone say, and the others laughed. The torch went out and I lay under the platform until my heart stopped banging and the truck roared away into the night.

This was the most dangerous plan I'd ever done, and already things were going wrong. I prayed that Billy would be waiting on the beach, that he'd seen the disappearing tail-lights, heard the rumble of the truck. I'd told him that the signal would be the sound of shattering glass. Would he listen for it? Would he come then or would he chicken out again?

Quiet as Archimedes's leopard, I crept beside the

Carousel of War and Peace. I passed the pinto pony with the moon on his stirrups and the wind in his mane, and I wished that Tia was sitting there in her red coat. I moved on; past the Dodgem Cars and the tin ducks in Sideshow Alley, and still she wasn't there. Then I rounded the corner and saw the other truck nosed right up to the refreshment pavilion, and suddenly I knew where Tia would be.

The lights of the truck beamed a spotlight on the stage, and I stood in the shadows watching her dance. I can't remember if it was the smoke or the movement I noticed first. When I turned, I saw the orange glow on the end of a cigarette and I knew Tia and I weren't the only ones there. Two soldiers were sitting in the corner on plastic chairs, and another one was standing behind them. I pressed my back against the broken lattice wall but they were all watching Tia and hadn't seen me. Then the soldiers who were sitting down started to clap, but not in the way people do when they think you've done an excellent job. They clapped slow and loud. Gradually, like the ballerina in the music box, Tia stopped dancing, as though she couldn't hear the music inside herself any more.

One of the soldiers who'd been clapping said something. When the man standing behind him walked towards the truck, I saw it was the skinny young soldier. He opened the door and reached inside and music came belting out. Then he lit a cigarette and disappeared himself into the dark. The others clapped louder and louder until Tia started dancing again, only this time she wasn't dancing to please herself; she was dancing to please the two soldiers in front of her.

One of them got up on the stage and ripped his camouflage shirt off. He whirled it around his head and then threw it on the ground and starting dancing with Tia. He undid the buckle on his belt, snaked it out and cracked it like a whip. The other one got up then and pulled Tia hard against him. She put her hands on his chest and tried to push him away but he laughed and pulled her back and kissed her roughly. I thought about the kiss that Tia had given me for free and I wondered if the soldier knew that she was only fifteen. I had to stop myself from screaming when I saw what they did to her next.

I didn't know how to help Tia. The only thing that was going to save us was the truck. But Billy wasn't there to start it. I backed slowly away from the pavilion, crept behind the truck and down the side towards the open door. Then I saw something unbelievable: a set of keys hanging in the ignition. I knew straight away what to do. I'd steal the keys and then lead the soldiers away from Tia.

I knew they had guns, but there wasn't time to come up with something better. All Tia had to do was hide and wait for us. I'd double back to the beach and find the others once I'd given the soldiers the slip. Sooner or later they'd leave, and when they did, we'd be waiting to drive away.

My muscles tensed for a quick getaway. I closed my hand around the keys, turned them, ever so slowly, and pulled.

Instantly, the lights died, the music stopped. Soldiers burst through the door of the pavilion, shouting, pulling their clothes on, grabbing their guns. I ran, dodging between the rides, twisting and turning in and out of shadows and moonlight, through the hall of mirrors – fat boy, thin boy, short boy, tall – rolling under the shooting gallery, bullets ripping through the tin ducks, real bullets. Stay away, Billy, don't come, not yet. Behind the Dodgem Cars, lungs on fire. Lose them, double back, into the House of Horrors. I crawled under the platform to Dracula and the ghosts, lay still and prayed that Tia had got away, that Billy, Max and Sixpence were safe.

Silence, silence except for the thudding of my heart. Then Tia screamed and I flew to the spy holes. She was on her knees, her hands pressed together in front of her like she was praying. The soldier behind her jerked her head towards him with a handful of her hair. I saw the pistol in his hand and I knew he was waiting for me to show myself.

All Tia had done was what they wanted, and all I had done was watch. Surely they weren't going to kill us. Couldn't they see we were children? Didn't they know we had no weapons? Maybe if I gave them their keys back? Was that a fair trade: our freedom for Tia's life? I didn't know, I only knew that I couldn't let Tia die.

I burst from the House of Horrors. Tia saw me first.

'Run, Skip, run!' she shouted.

I threw the keys as hard as I could. They curved up into the midnight blue. For a split second the soldier looked up as they tumbled towards him like a falling star. In a single, swift movement, Tia rose on her knees, arched her arms over her head and drove her fists into his chest. He staggered, then crumpled and fell face down. Tia started towards me. She didn't see the other soldier taking aim from behind the broken lattice, or the young one near the truck. Too late, my scream ripped through the night, jagged as saw-teeth between the shots.

The young soldier rolled his comrade onto his back and stared for a few seconds at the knife handle sticking out of his chest. Then he stood up, dropped his gun next to the other soldier, the one he'd shot, and ran behind the pavilion, vomiting all the way.

I flung myself down beside Tia, remembering the wrongness I had felt on the morning Billy discovered his knife was missing. It was only a small knife with a handle made of shell. It was blunt from opening tins and picking locks and other useful things. I didn't think you could kill a man with a knife like that. But Tia did. She did it so the rest of us could get away.

Lights blazed at the hotel, engines revved, doors slammed and sirens howled. I grabbed the keys off the ground, but what to do? There was only me. I'd never driven anything. Where was Billy? Where were Max and Sixpence? Would they come? Should I leave Tia and try to find them; come back later?

Trucks wound down the corkscrew hill. The young soldier stopped throwing up. He'd seen me.

Then Billy walked out from behind the carousel with Sixpence on his back and Max beside him, and everything we needed for our one last chance.

'Get in, Max!' I hissed. 'We've got to leave. Now!' I didn't want him to look at Tia and the dead soldiers.

Billy and me put our hands together underneath Tia and moved her across to the truck, but we couldn't lift her high enough to put her in the back.

The other trucks were closing in.

I wanted to be with Max. I wanted Billy to drive

us away before it was too late, but I couldn't leave Tia there.

I saw the young soldier running towards us. Three guns lay on the ground between us. Billy's eyes met mine, our hands gripped tight underneath Tia. His face looked afraid, like my heart. Then the soldier did something I never thought he'd do. He took Tia in his arms, but not like the other soldiers; he took her from us with gentle hands, lifted her up and laid her down in the dark next to Max. He took off his big coat and put it over her. After he helped Billy up, he put his hand out to me and I put the golden keys into it because I knew he'd figured out that he was on the Third Side.

21

Pennyweight Flat

Sandbags scattered and barricades splintered as the truck hurtled through the first checkpoint. We lay low in the back as bullets sizzled past us. The soldier took a crazy, twisted route, nosing through narrow streets in silent suburbs with no streetlights and no headlights. Our truck driver was a murderer. They were looking for him because he did the worst thing: he killed a comrade; killed him for a beautiful fifteen-year-old girl who stuck a blunt pocketknife into a soldier's chest so that her baby daughter and her friends could go free. He did it because he was on the Third Side, that didn't believe in war.

I wondered if it had been Tia or me that he'd killed, would the others have tried to hunt him down? I wondered if he'd been sent to war, like Old Thomas was, or maybe he was like my dad and thought it would be an adventure. All I knew, with every part of me, was that he was in a war he didn't want to be in and no one was going to tell him he could go home.

I held the torch while Billy wrapped Tia in torn sheets to stop the bleeding. But with each new strip of rag he added we saw the blood soak through, redder than her coat. We covered her with the soldier's coat again and then Billy and I lay, one each side of her, trying to keep her warm, trying to stop her from moving while the truck swerved and swayed through unfamiliar streets. Sixpence slept on my chest, warm and soft and alive in her pouch, and Billy held Max in his arms. I closed my eyes tight and tried to hear the music that was inside Tia, but all I could hear was the sound of her lungs trying to squeeze her heavy red breath in and out, in and out.

Through the night we drove in a tangle of waking and sleeping, nightmares from hell and holy white dreams. In my waking I thought about the soldier and wondered if he knew where he was going. I remembered his pale, sweating face and his shaking hands when I gave him the keys. I saw Billy sit up like a grey ghost and look out into the darkness. He bent low over Tia and made the sign of the cross the way he had on poor Bradley Clark.

I wanted to tell him he was wrong, that he'd made a mistake, that Tia was still alive. But I knew it was only my own body heat making her warm.

Billy took Old Thomas's cigarette from inside his coat. He struck a match and the tiny flame flickered and died. I smelt the smoke and saw it drift away. After he finished his cigarette, Billy tapped on the window that separated us from the driver and I felt the truck slow down. The cabin door opened and Billy passed Max down to the soldier, then he crawled back on his hands and knees to me.

'Skip!' I heard him whisper, and smelt the sour smell of cigarettes on his breath. I knew he wanted me to get in the front with him and Max, but I kept my eyes shut. 'Wake up, Skip.' Billy shook my arm. I opened my eyes a crack and looked at him. 'We've given them the slip,' he said. 'They'll never find us now. Come on, come inside the cabin, it's warmer there.'

I shook my head, so Billy took Sixpence with him and left me there.

Before the truck drove off again the light came on in the cabin and I heard Billy talking. I couldn't hear what he was saying, but I guessed he was telling the soldier which way to go.

I combed the knots out of Tia's hair with my fingers, and told her I'd keep my promise to take care of Sixpence, and I cried. Then I lay down and thought about the slap-up meal and the wishbone, and I wished I'd tried harder and pulled stronger, because I would have made the right wish.

I don't know how long it was before I felt the truck slow down and turn off the highway. The wheels crunched over gravel. I looked through the window in the back of the cabin and out through the front windscreen. The soldier turned the truck's lights on and I saw a small white bridge. He slowed the truck down even more until I thought we were going to stop. We rolled forward and the planks of the bridge groaned as we drove slowly across. Then the headlights shone on a sign that said Moonlight Flat. The soldier flicked the lights off again and the truck crawled slowly up the road until we reached the top of a small hill. A sign said Pennyweight Flat Children's Cemetery.

A pennyweight is a measure of gold. If you had a piece of gold that weighed one pennyweight it would be about the size of a small fingernail. This means that a pennyweight of gold is a tiny treasure. It doesn't matter how big or how small a treasure is, it's still a treasure.

At the Pennyweight Flat Children's Cemetery the ground is full of treasure. Miners came there to find gold in eighteen hundred and fifty-one. But over the next six years, two hundred people got buried at the cemetery. A lot of them were the miners' babies and children, and some of them were the mums and dads. This is true; I read it on the sign I saw when I got out of the truck.

I climbed out first, and then Billy got out with Sixpence, and the soldier lifted Max down onto the stony ground. Next he lifted Tia out and carried her through the small silver gate. We followed him, in single file, between the mossy rocks that the miners had arranged around their most precious treasures. Max and me spread the red coat on the ground and the soldier laid Tia down beneath the stars. We opened a bottle of water and washed away her blood, and when we were done we sat back and let the moon shine itself all over her, and we saw that Tia was full of light. Billy said that when we die the darkness leaves us.

'We're pure and perfect then,' he said, 'the way we are when we're born.'

Max and me spread our blankets on the ground and we laid ourselves down beside Tia. We held her hands and looked up at the millions of stars. The night was hushed and holy and we stayed with Tia until morning came, and we were not afraid.

By sunrise the soldier had scraped a hole in the ground for Tia. Billy unwrapped his Hohner. He curled his fingers around it and closed his eyes and played the blessing song. When it was over we lay Tia in the ground, among the fingernails of gold.

22

The most
important thing

After we'd said goodbye to Tia we went back to the truck and climbed into the front with the soldier. Billy looked at the book of maps and pointed out which way we should go.

The wheels hummed lullabies on the liquorice road and Max and Sixpence were soon asleep. Sixpence had learnt to suck her thumb, her cheeks had cooled and the rattle in her chest had almost gone. I rested my chin on her fairy-floss hair and closed my eyes.

This time my head was empty of dreams. When I woke again, a long time later, the truck had stopped by the side of the road. I looked out and saw a dirt track winding through the tall and bending grass. At the end was an old white house.

'Max,' I said, 'wake up, Max!'

Max put his fingers under his glasses and rubbed his eyes, and then he looked out the window. 'See, I told you!' he said.

Billy opened the door and elbowed me in the ribs. 'Out you get.'

I climbed down and parted the grass with my hands, searching for a small white post. When I found it, I checked the letters and numbers I'd written on my hand. I had to be sure. The others watched me from the truck and I yelled out, 'Chuck us Dad's coat, Billy!'

He tossed the coat through the window and I opened the gate and let the soldier drive through. Sixpence waved her starfish hands and smiled her toothless smile and I thought about the promise I'd made to Tia. I rode the rusty gate back to its leaning post and watched the truck for a while, bumping slowly towards the house in the distance. I put my hands up to the sky and looked with both my eyes at the same time. I saw the way the light fell and where the shadows lay. Then I chased the truck along the dusty track through Gulliver's Meadows and my heart was a dancing red kite.

One day I'll give the silver necklace to Sixpence and I'll tell her about Tia. I'll tell her how beautiful she was and how brave. And I'll tell her the most important thing of all: that her mother loved her better than her life.

About the author

Glenda Millard has written picture books, short stories and novels for children and young adults. She began thinking about the main character for this book after noticing a newspaper headline 'Urban Tribes', and she wondered what life would be like for a young homeless boy, living with people thrown together in circumstances beyond their control.

Glenda is fascinated by the way chance plays its part in our lives. She says: 'Nearly forty years after I left school, I discovered that one of my high school teachers had restored a carousel. Having always loved carousels, I was intrigued and spent a wonderful day with my ex-teacher, learning about the very labour-intensive process of restoring carousels. Subsequently, I went to Geelong and rode on that carousel. Later, on a wet, grey day in June, I went to St Kilda and rode the carousel at Luna Park. I wrote a story about a carousel horse, which will soon be published as a picture book. And when I started writing A *Small Free Kiss in the Dark*, the memory of my carousel ride on that misty day in June came back to me and seemed a perfect setting for my novel. By situating much of the story in a fun park, I hoped to juxtapose the location with the events that took place there. While the backdrop for this story is war, my intention was to capture the indomitable nature of hope, even in dire situations.'

Glenda Millard lives in the Goldfields region of Central Victoria, Australia. She left school at fifteen after a childhood filled with stories but only became a published writer later in life, once she had two grown-up children. Her novels and picture books have won many accolades and awards in her home country and she conducts creative writing workshops in both poetry and prose. Glenda also loves fly fishing.

Teacher's notes for this title are available. Please email info@oldbarnbooks.com